The Mr Meddle
Stories

The Mr Meddle Stories

Enid Blyton

Illustrations by Diana Catchpole

BLOOMSBURY
CHILDREN'S
BOOKS

First published by Parragon Publishing in 1999
Queen Street House, 4/5 Queen Street, Bath BA1 1HE

Mister Meddle's Mischief was first published by Newnes in 1940
First published by Bloomsbury Publishing Plc in 1997
38 Soho Square, London, W1V 5DF
Merry Mr Meddle was first published by George Newnes in 1954
Mister Meddle's Muddles was first published by Newnes in 1950
First published by Bloomsbury Publishing Plc in 1998
38 Soho Square, London, W1V 5DF

Enid Blyton™

The moral right of the author has been asserted
A CIP catalogue record of this book is available from the
British Library

ISBN 1 84164 093 X

Printed in Scotland by Caledonian International Book Manufacturing Ltd

10 9 8 7 6 5 4 3 2 1

Mr Meddle's
Mischief

Mr Meddle's Mischief

Enid Blyton
Illustrations by Diana Catchpole

BLOOMSBURY
CHILDREN'S
BOOKS

Contents

Chapter 1

Mister Meddle's Morning

Mister Meddle was a pixie who couldn't mind his own business. He was forever poking his long nose into other people's houses, and meddling with whatever they were doing.

One day he felt more meddlesome than usual, so he ran round to Dame Gladsome's. She was very busy that morning, but as soon as she saw Mister Meddle's nose round the door she flew to shut it!

'I've come to help you,' said Meddle crossly.

'Oh, I'm much too busy to be bothered with your help!' said Dame Gladsome, and she turned the key in the lock.

Mister Meddle frowned and went to Old Man Twinkle, who was on the top of a ladder beside his big bookcase, turning out all his old books and dusting them.

'I'd like to help you,' said Meddle, putting his head in at the window. He gave Old Man Twinkle such a fright that he fell off his ladder and bounced on to the table, sending his books up into the air.

Meddle decided not to wait and see what Old Man Twinkle said. He ran off and came to a neat little house on the top of the hill. It belonged to Mother Heyho. Meddle didn't know her very well. He knocked at her door.

Mother Heyho opened it. She had a handkerchief tied round her head and a duster in her hand.

'Good morning,' said Meddle politely. 'Is there anything I can do for you? I happened to be passing, and as I had nothing much to do today, I wondered if I could be any help to you.'

'How nice of you!' said Mother Heyho, who didn't know what a nuisance Mister Meddle could be. 'Well, I badly want some butter and some eggs. Could you fetch some for me?'

Meddle was off like a shot. He went to the dairy, got the butter and eggs, and ran back with them. Mother Heyho opened the door. Meddle rushed in, but unfortunately he didn't notice that Mother Heyho had just polished the floor. He slid on a mat, turned head-over-heels – and the bag of eggs went flying to the ceiling and came down, smack, on Mother Heyho's head!

Mother Heyho was not at all pleased. Meddle put the butter carefully down on a chair and rubbed his bruises.

'Anyway, the butter's not broken, like the eggs,' he said.

'Don't be silly,' said Mother Heyho, trying

to get the eggs off her hair. 'Butter doesn't break – but if it did, you'd have broken it! Now I shall have to wash my hair.'

'I'll help you,' said Meddle eagerly. He fetched a bowl for Mother Heyho and filled it full of water. Mother Heyho began to wash her hair. 'Get me some more hot water,' she said. 'There's some in that kettle. Put it into a jug for me to pour over my hair.'

Meddle emptied the water into a jug. Then he thought it would be very helpful if he poured the water over Mother Heyho's hair himself. So he tilted up the jug and poured.

'Oooh! Ow! Oooh!' yelled poor Mother Heyho, jumping almost up to the ceiling in fright. 'It's boiling hot, you silly fellow! I'm cooked, I'm cooked!'

Meddle was horrified. He looked at Mother Heyho jumping round the kitchen, holding her hot head. He ran to the tap and drew some cold water. He threw it over Mother Heyho's hair.

'Ooooh! It's ice-cold!' shouted Mother Heyho. 'Stop it! Leave me alone!'

Meddle tried to put the jug on the table and just missed it. Crash! It fell on to the floor and broke.

'My best milk-jug, oh, my best milk-jug!' wept Mother Heyho, in despair.

'Sorry,' said Meddle. 'I'll get some glue and mend it.'

He ran to the store cupboard and found a little bottle of glue. Then back he went to mend the milk-jug. He put the glue on the table and picked up the milk-jug bits. But just as he was pressing them together his hand slipped – and he knocked the glue-bottle off the table! The glue poured out on to the chair, the table, and the floor! Oh, what a mess!

Mother Heyho was busy drying her hair and didn't see what had happened. Meddle picked up the glue-bottle, but he couldn't pick up the glue!

The next thing that happened, of course, was that Meddle stepped straight into the sticky glue! His shoes stuck to the floor, and when he tried to get away his feet slipped out of his shoes, and there he was, dancing about in his socks! And, of course, the next thing he did was to dance right on to the glue again! This time, when he tried to get out of it his socks came off, and there he was, in his bare feet!

Mother Heyho put her towel down at that moment and saw Meddle rushing about in bare feet. She was most astonished.

'Why have you taken your shoes and socks off?' she asked. 'Do you think you're going to bed or something?'

Mother Heyho put her towel down on the gluey table, and glared at Meddle. She was getting tired of him. When she tried to pick the towel up she couldn't – it had stuck! She pulled in surprise.

'Let *me* help!' said Meddle at once, and he gave an enormous tug at the towel. It came up – and so did the table! Meddle sat down hurriedly on the floor, and the table fell on top of him, and a corner of it went on to Mother Heyho's toe.

How she yelled! She danced round the kitchen on one leg, holding her toe, whilst Meddle pushed away the table and tried to get up. The gluey towel had got round his neck and he couldn't get it off.

'Oh, you wicked fellow!' cried Mother Heyho. 'Look at all the mess and muddle you've made! Look at all the damage you've done! Now don't you dare to do another thing! Sit down and don't dare to move!'

Mother Heyho looked so fierce that Mister Meddle thought he had better do as he was told. So he sat down, squish, on a chair! But Mother Heyho only yelled at him all the more.

'Oh, you bad fellow! Oh, you silly pixie! Now you've sat on my butter! Get up, get up! You're sitting on my butter, I tell you! You've broken my eggs – and messed my hair – and nearly cooked my head – and broken my milk-jug – and got glue over everything –

and hurt my toe – and now you must sit on my butter! What else will you do, I'd like to know?'

Mister Meddle was frightened. He got up off the butter, and tried to go to the door in his bare feet. He could see Dame Gladsome and Old Man Twinkle going by outside.

'I can see two friends of mine,' he said to Mother Heyho. 'I must go.'

'Well, I'll help you to go!' said Mother Heyho fiercely, and she caught up her big broom. Swish – swish – swish! She swept poor Meddle right off his feet, and he shot down

the garden path and through the gate in a fearful hurry. He landed just under Old Man Twinkle's feet and gave him a fright.

'My goodness, it's Mister Meddle again!' said Dame Gladsome. 'Is this the way you usually come out of a house, my dear Meddle? It seems very sudden.'

Mister Meddle didn't answer. He rushed home in his bare feet, and got into a hot bath to get off all the glue. But it won't be long before he meddles again with somebody. He just simply can't help it!

Chapter 2

Mister Meddle
and the Conjurer

Did you ever hear how Mister Meddle meddled with a conjurer one day? You didn't? – well, I'll tell you.

Now, you know, at some parties there is a conjurer who does all kinds of marvellous magic things. Well, once Meddle was invited to one of these parties, and he went, dressed up in his best suit, and feeling all excited.

There was a lovely tea – and afterwards there was to be the conjurer, doing magic tricks. Meddle didn't say a word all through his tea, because he was wondering and wondering how the conjurer would do his magic. He guessed it must be because of his magic wand.

'Please go and play Nuts in May whilst I

get the room ready for the conjurer,' said Mrs Twinkle, who was giving the party. So every one went into the next room, and soon they were singing, 'Here we come gathering Nuts in May!'

But Mister Meddle wasn't. No – he had slipped into the tiny room where he had seen the conjurer put his coat and hat and bag, just to see if he could find anything interesting!

The bag was open! Some of the things were unpacked. The conjurer was not there. He was helping Mrs Twinkle to arrange the chairs, so Meddle had the little room to himself.

He looked for the magic wand. It was in the bag! Meddle carefully took it out and looked at it. It was a thin silver wand, and it felt strangely heavy in his hands.

Meddle was suddenly full of excitement. He would use the wand and see if he could make it do some magic for him! So he waved it in the air and wished!

'I wish for a sack of gold!'

There was a thud beside him – and a great brown sack appeared, tied up at the neck. Meddle trembled with joy. Oooh! The wand

was really magic. Look at this enormous
sack!

'I must hide it outside where no one will
see it!' said Meddle. So he dragged it outside
and hid it behind the wall. Then he crept
into the little room again and picked up the
silver wand.

'What shall I wish for this time?' he wondered. He looked down at his shoes, and saw
that they were very muddy from going out

into the garden. That would never do! So Meddle waved the wand and wished once more.

'I wish for a beautiful pair of golden shoes on my feet!' Something flew off his feet – and his old shoes were gone! Something clapped themselves *on* his feet – and bless us all, there was Meddle wearing the most beautiful pair of real gold shoes, shining and glittering like the sun!

'Gracious!' said Meddle. 'I *am* getting on! I'll wish for something else now, before the conjurer comes back. I can hear him talking to Mrs Twinkle.

'I wish for my larder at home to be filled with all sorts of things to eat – treacle puddings, jam rolls, chocolate cakes, ice-creams, and anything else that's nice!' he wished. Then he heard the conjurer coming and he slipped out of the room and ran to where the others were still playing Nuts in May.

Now, when the conjurer was standing in front of everyone, later on, looking at all the guests sitting in their chairs, he picked up his magic wand to do some magic. And as soon as he picked it up and waved it, he knew someone had been meddling with it!

How did he know? Oh, quite easily! You see, when a wand is full of magic, it is very heavy – but it gets lighter as it is used. And Meddle had used it three times, so that now it was very light indeed.

The conjurer looked in astonishment at his wand. Then he glared at all the people in front of him.

'Someone,' he said, 'SOMEONE has been using my wand. The goodness is gone out of it. *Who* has done this?'

Nobody answered. Meddle was dreadfully frightened. He hadn't guessed that the conjurer would find out. How he wished he hadn't meddled with the magic wand now!

'I say again,' said the conjurer, in a very angry voice, '*WHO* has used my wand? I will give them this one chance – and I warn them that if they do not come forward and tell me, they will be punished, and will be very sorry indeed.'

Meddle sat quite still in his chair. *He* wasn't going to own up. Not he! How could the conjurer punish him if he didn't know who it was that had used the wand?

'Very well,' said the conjurer. 'I will say no more. But the one who has used my magic will be very sorry before the night has gone.'

The party went on. Mister Meddle didn't enjoy it a bit, because he knew he should not have touched the wand, and he knew that he certainly should have owned up when the conjurer had spoken about it.

All the same, he was delighted to think he had a sack of gold, golden shoes on his feet, and a cupboard full of the most delicious food at home!

When the time came to say goodbye, Meddle slipped away first, dragging with him on his shoulder his enormous sack. He went down the darkest lanes so that he should not meet anyone.

The sack was terribly heavy. He had to keep putting it down and resting. Really, he had never known such a heavy sack in all his life! He would be very rich with all that gold!

Suddenly his feet began to hurt him. His golden shoes were heavy and tight, and they began to press on his toes and heels in a very painful manner.

'I'll take them off and put them in my pocket,' thought Mister Meddle. 'Then they won't hurt me. I can easily walk in my socks.'

But he couldn't get the golden shoes off!

They just simply would *not* come off! He tried and he tried, but it was no use at all.

So there was nothing for it but to go on wearing them, though poor Meddle groaned and grunted at every step! At last he got home. He dragged the sack into his kitchen and lighted his lamp. He took a knife and cut the string that bound up the neck of the sack.

He put in his hand to get out the gold – but oh, what a dreadful, dreadful disappointment! The sack was full of nothing but big stones! The magic had gone out of it and the gold had turned to nasty, heavy stones. Poor Meddle – he had dragged stones all the way home!

He sat down to take off his shoes, which were hurting him more than ever. But no – it was impossible to take them off. Meddle began to feel frightened. The gold had turned to stones – and the shoes wouldn't come off! He didn't like it at all!

'Never mind – perhaps I'll find all those delicious things in my cupboard that I wished for,' he thought. 'I'm hungry now – I'll have a few!'

He went to the cupboard and opened it,

half afraid that he wouldn't find anything there. But on the shelves were the treacle puddings, the chocolate cakes, the jam rolls, and many other things he had wished for. Good!

He took down an ice-cream and fetched a spoon. He put a spoonful into his mouth – but, good gracious me, he spat it out again at once! It burnt his tongue! Yes, it really did! Meddle stared at the ice-cream as if he couldn't believe his eyes. How could ice burn? He must have been mistaken. He tried again. But this time the ice-cream burnt his tongue so much that he screamed and ran to get some cold water.

Then he tried the treacle pudding – but the treacle tasted like salt and was horrible. He bit a chocolate biscuit, but it tasted of cardboard and he couldn't swallow it. He licked the jam off a tart, but it was made of pepper and made him sneeze and choke till the tears came into his eyes!

'Oh, it's too bad, it's too bad!' said Meddle, in despair. 'All the magic has gone wrong. Why didn't I own up when I had the chance? Here I've tired myself out dragging a heavy sack of stones all the way home – and

my feet are almost crippled with these dreadfully tight shoes – and now I've burnt my tongue, and tasted all sorts of horrible things that look as nice as can be!'

He decided to go to bed – but still he couldn't get his shoes off, and they seemed to be growing tighter and tighter and tighter. It was dreadful!

At last, in despair, Mister Meddle went out into the dark night with his lantern, to go back to Mrs Twinkle's and ask if the conjurer was still there. He really, really must get these shoes off his feet! He would have to confess – and say he was sorry. He really *was* sorry, too. It was a dreadful thing to meddle with someone else's magic.

The conjurer was staying the night at Mrs Twinkle's. He didn't seem a bit surprised to see the trembling Meddle. He stared at him without a smile.

'I was expecting you,' he said sternly. 'Meddlers are always punished.'

'Please forgive me,' begged Meddle. 'My sack of gold turned to stones. My larder of good things cannot be eaten – and my feet are so tired of these shoes.'

'You must wear them for three days,' said the conjurer, looking at them. 'I cannot take them off, for the magic is too strong. As for the things in your larder, throw them away, for they will be of no use to anyone.'

Poor Meddle! He limped home, crying. He threw away all the lovely things in his larder, and he emptied his sack of stones at the bottom of the garden. Then he went to bed with his golden shoes on!

And for three days he had to wear them. Then they became looser and he took them off and threw them down the well. Horrible things! He wasn't going to keep them!

'That's taught me never to meddle again!' said Mister Meddle solemnly. 'Never – never – never!'

And he didn't meddle with anything for a whole month. But after that – well, I'm afraid he forgot again. That's another story!

Chapter 3

Mister Meddle
at the Station

It happened once that Mister Meddle went
to the railway station to see his old friends
Pippin and his wife off by train.

Now Pippin wasn't at all pleased to see
Meddle, for he knew what muddles people
got into when Meddle was anywhere about!
So he just nodded to Meddle, and tried to
pretend that he was far too busy to bother
with him.

'Pippin!' cried Meddle. 'Are you very
busy?'

'Very,' said Pippin. 'I've lots of things to do
– tickets to get – luggage to see to – the right
train to find – haven't a minute to spare,
Meddle. Goodbye!'

'My dear old friend, if you're as busy as all

that, I must really help you!' cried Meddle. 'Now – let me get the tickets for you! Where are you going to?'

'We're going to Lemon Village,' said Pippin. 'But I can get the tickets. Don't you bother, Meddle.'

'No bother, no bother at all!' cried Mister Meddle. He held out his hand for the money and Pippin gave him some.

'I want a ticket for my parrot too,' he said. 'I've got it in a cage here.' Meddle rushed off. There were a lot of people by the ticket-office waiting their turn to get tickets. Meddle took up his place and waited. At last he got to the ticket-man.

'Where to?' asked the man impatiently. Mister Meddle frowned. Now where did Pippin say he and his wife were going to?

'Er – er – two tickets for Orange Town, and an extra ticket for a canary,' said Meddle at last. He paid for the tickets and rushed back. On the way he thought he would try and find out what platform the train left from.

'Where's the train for Orange Town?' asked Meddle when a porter passed.

'Number eight platform, and the train

leaves at five minutes past eleven!' said the porter.

'Good gracious!' cried Meddle in alarm. 'Why, Pippin said it left at a *quarter* past eleven – he'll miss it! I wonder whether he has got his luggage there yet.'

Meddle looked round, and nearby he saw a pile of luggage, with a canary's cage set on top. 'That must be their luggage!' he cried. 'Good! I'll see to it for them! Hie, porter!'

A porter hurried up. 'Take this luggage to platform number eight, and put it on the five-past-eleven train to Orange Town,' said Meddle, in a grand voice. He did love seeing to things.

The porter stared. 'But a lady told me to leave it here just now whilst she went to get a cup of tea,' he said.

'My good man, do as you're told!' said Meddle. 'Look – here are the tickets – one for the canary too – now just do as you are told!'

The porter put the things on his trolley, for he thought that if Meddle had the tickets he must own the luggage. Off he trundled to the train on platform number eight, and put the things neatly into a carriage.

Meddle looked about for his friends. They would certainly miss the train if they didn't hurry! He would buy them some chocolate to eat on the train. That was a good idea. So he ran to a machine, put in ten pence – and got out two boxes of matches, which he felt quite sure were chocolate! Really, Meddle!

He still couldn't see Pippin and Mrs Pippin. And then at last he caught sight of them in the carriage of a train nearby! 'You're in the wrong train!' shouted Meddle. 'Hie, Pippin, your train is on platform eight!'

Pippin looked alarmed. He jumped out of the carriage and helped Mrs Pippin out too. He called to a porter to bring their things from the carriage and ran to Meddle.

'Are you sure?' he said. 'We did ask if this was right and we were told it was.'

'You leave things to me,' said Meddle, importantly. 'I've arranged everything. I've got your tickets for you – and some chocolate. Come along at once.'

Meddle hurried Mr and Mrs Pippin to platform eight. It was almost time for that train to go. He found the carriage where the luggage and the canary cage were, and put Pippin and his wife in. Behind them hurried the porter with their things from the other train, a big parrot cage on top.

'But this looks as if somebody else had taken this carriage,' said Pippin, looking round at the luggage already there, and the canary's cage on the rack above their heads.

'Here is some chocolate for you both,' said Meddle, and he pushed the boxes of matches into Pippin's hand. Pippin looked at the matches.

'Are you quite mad, Meddle?' he said. 'These are matches! We can't eat those!'

'Oh dear!' said Meddle – and then he suddenly caught sight of the porter with all the luggage belonging to the Pippins. The man pushed Meddle aside and began to put the luggage into the carriage.

'My good man, this carriage is already full of people and luggage,' said Meddle grandly. 'Take it away.'

'But, Meddle, that's *our* luggage,' said Mrs Pippin, who was getting very tired of Meddle. 'Of course the man must put it in. We don't want to leave it behind!'

'*Your* luggage!' said Meddle, in a surprised voice. 'But I don't understand. Surely all this is yours that I got the other porter to put here – and see, there's your canary cage!'

'Canary cage!' snorted Pippin. 'Don't be silly, Meddle. We haven't any canary. We've a parrot. Look out – here comes the cage. Mind the parrot doesn't peck you!'

The parrot put its curved beak through the bars of its cage and tweaked Meddle's arm. He yelled.

'Don't! Oh, I say, Pippin, this is very strange. All the other luggage that I told the other porter to put in here must belong to somebody else then! Oh dear!'

The engine whistled. A ticket-collector came. 'Can I see your tickets, please?' he asked. 'The train is just going.'

Meddle gave Pippin the tickets he had bought and Pippin showed them to the collector. 'Orange Town!' said the man. 'Change at Holly Corner.'

'But we're not going to Orange Town, we're going to Lemon Village!' cried Pippin in alarm.

'Not in this train,' said the collector. 'It goes the other way! The Lemon Village train starts from platform number two in ten minutes' time. Hop out quickly!'

Pippin and Mrs Pippin hopped out and threw their luggage on to the platform. They took the parrot from the rack just in time, for the train shook itself and then steamed off to Holly Corner! All the other luggage, canary and all, went off in the empty carriage.

'Go away, Meddle!' shouted Pippin angrily. 'Go away! You've made enough muddles to last us for a month! I shall change the tickets, and find my own train again. Taking tickets to Orange Town indeed, when we wanted Lemon Village – and buying a canary's ticket when we wanted a parrot's! Here, take your matches – *we* don't want them!'

Biff-smack! The two boxes hit Meddle on the nose. Then Pippin and his wife hurried to platform number two with their luggage, and Pippin sent the porter to change the tickets. There was just time!

Meddle felt very hurt. He thought he had better vanish away – but what was this? A porter came up to him with a large, fierce-looking lady.

'Here's the fellow that told me to put your luggage and your canary into the train for Orange Town,' said the porter. 'They've gone now, Madam.'

'Oh, they have, have they?' said the large fierce lady, and she took Mister Meddle by his long nose. 'I suppose you are one of these meddling, interfering people who just make trouble for everybody! Well, you come along with me and we'll see what the station-master has to say to you!'

The station-master said a lot, and in the end Mister Meddle had to buy himself a ticket to Orange Town and go and fetch the luggage and the canary he had sent there. He felt very upset indeed.

'I'll never bother to help anyone again!' he vowed. 'I really – really – won't!'

But he just can't keep that long nose of his out of other people's business!

Chapter 4

Mister Meddle
Goes Out to Tea

Once Mister Meddle went out to tea with Sally Simple. Sally didn't know Meddle as well as most people did, or she might not have asked him.

He arrived at Sally's house dressed in his best. He was early, and Sally Simple was not quite ready.

'Oh, never mind, never mind!' said Meddle, beaming. 'Just give me a few jobs to do for you about the house, dear Sally, and I'll be quite happy. I love helping people.'

Sally Simple thought what a nice fellow Mister Meddle was. 'Well,' she said, 'you might feed the goldfish for me, if you will, and you might put some more food into the canary's cage.'

'Certainly, certainly!' said Meddle. 'Anything else? Those jobs won't take me long.'

'Well – would you put the kettle on to boil?' asked Sally. 'And would you like to go and pick some ripe strawberries for tea? They are lovely just now.'

'I'd love to!' said Meddle, rubbing his hands in delight. 'Strawberries! Ha! Just what I like. Have you any cream?'

'There's a jar of cream in the larder,' said Sally. 'Now, I'll just go upstairs and put on a clean blouse. I won't be long. You'll find the birdseed and the goldfish food in the cupboard over there.'

Sally ran upstairs, thinking it was a real pleasure to meet anyone so friendly and helpful as Mister Meddle.

Meddle looked at the two goldfish swimming in their little bowl. He looked at the canary. 'I'll give you your dinner!' he said. 'Pretty things, pretty things!'

'Tweet!' said the canary, but the goldfish said nothing at all.

Meddle went to the cupboard. There were two packets there – one of goldfish food, which was ants' eggs, or rather ant-grub cocoons, and the other was canary-seed.

What did silly old Meddle do but scatter birdseed on the top of the goldfish bowl, and give the ants' eggs to the canary! The canary put its head on one side and pecked up the eggs. It liked them. But the goldfish didn't like the birdseed at all.

'Not hungry, I suppose,' said Meddle, watching the goldfish swimming about. 'You haven't snapped at a single bit of your food, fish! Now, what else was I to do? Oh – put the kettle on to boil, of course!'

Meddle took up the kettle and set it on the stove. He didn't think of filling it with water. He just put it there to boil – without water!

'Now for the strawberries!' he said. He took a basket and went out into the garden. There were heaps of lovely red strawberries. It didn't take Meddle long to fill his basket. He went back to the house, whistling merrily.

He put the strawberries on a chair, and went to look for the cream. There was a jar in the cupboard full of yellow cream. Meddle emptied some into a jug and set it on the table. He didn't know that it was furniture cream that he had taken out of the polish-jar! No – Meddle never thought of things like that!

Sally Simple came down looking very nice. She beamed at Meddle. 'Done all your jobs?' she asked.

'Yes,' said Meddle. 'I've fed the goldfish – look!'

Sally looked, and then she looked again. 'Do you usually feed goldfish with bird-seed?' she said, in rather an annoyed voice. 'Why did you do that, Mister Meddle? I suppose you thought it would make them sing.'

Meddle went red. He looked at the canary's cage, and so did Sally. 'And you've given the canary the ants' eggs,' she said. 'Well, well, Meddle, I did think you knew the difference between goldfish and canaries, but if you don't I suppose you just can't help it!'

'I *do* know the difference!' said Meddle.

'I shouldn't have thought you did then,' said Sally. 'Now, is the kettle boiling? It doesn't look as if it is – no steam is coming from its spout!'

'I put it on ages ago,' said Meddle.

Sally took it up from the stove. It felt very light indeed. Sally glared at Meddle. 'There's no water in it!' she cried. 'Did you expect a kettle to boil without water?'

'Er – no,' said Meddle, feeling very foolish.

'Oh, look! The kettle has got a hole burnt in the bottom now – all because you were silly enough to put it on without water in!' cried Sally crossly. 'What will you do next?'

'I'm very sorry,' said Meddle, and he sat down on a chair, feeling rather upset. And, of course, he chose the chair on which he had put the basket of strawberries! Squish, squash!

'That's right, Meddle – strawberries are

meant to be sat on, not eaten!' said Sally
scornfully. 'I suppose that's what you put
them there for – to sit on!'

'They're all right,' said Meddle, getting up
and looking at the squashed basket and
strawberries. 'Just a bit flattened, that's all.
We will be able to eat them all right.'

'Well, if you want to eat sat-on strawberries, you can,' said Sally. 'But I'm not
going to. Did you find the cream? Or did you
put out marmalade or something instead?'

'If you look in the jug, you'll see I put out

cream,' said Meddle, very much hurt. Sally looked into the jug. The cream looked a bit yellow to her. She smelt it – and she knew that Meddle had put out the furniture cream instead of the real cream. She smiled a little smile to herself.

'You are sure this cream will be all right with sat-on strawberries?' she asked.

'Perfectly all right,' said Meddle. He emptied the squashed strawberries on to a plate and poured the cream all over them. He scattered sugar on them too. Then he took up a spoon and began to eat.

He didn't like the first mouthful at all. Oh dear, what a dreadful taste! He took another – but no, he really couldn't eat it!

'I feel ill, Sally,' he said in a faint voice. 'I think I'll go home. Goodbye! I'll come to tea with you another day.'

'You may not be asked!' said Sally, and she shut the door behind Meddle.

Poor Mister Meddle! He didn't eat strawberries and cream again for a long time!

Chapter 5

Mister Meddle on the Farm

Did you ever hear how Mister Meddle went to visit his sister, the farmer's wife? It's a funny story, to be sure!

Dame Henny wasn't at all pleased to see Meddle. She knew what a dreadful fellow he was for getting into a fix. But as he was her brother she had to make him welcome.

'You've come on rather a busy day for me,' said Dame Henny. 'It's baking day, you see, so I'm afraid I shan't have much time to spare you, Meddle.'

'Oh, don't worry about that,' said Meddle. 'I'll help you. I can go and collect the eggs – and milk the cows – and feed the pigs – and . . .'

'Meddle, I'd rather you didn't do a single

47

thing!' said Dame Henny at once. 'You're no good on a farm at all. I don't believe you know the difference between a hen and a duck!'

Meddle was offended. He sat down and ate a piece of cake and drank a glass of milk without saying a word. Dame Henny hoped that he was so offended he would go home. But he didn't.

'I'll just show my silly sister that I know a lot more than she thinks,' he said to himself. 'I'll just show her!'

So out he went to look for eggs. But Dame Henny had already hunted in all the nests and had taken every one. However, in two coops by themselves were two hens sitting on twelve eggs each, hatching them into chicks.

Meddle didn't know they were hatching the eggs. He thought they had laid them all. 'Ha!' he said, pleased. 'Look at that! Twelve eggs in *this* nest that my sister hasn't seen – and, dear me, twelve in this one! Oh! You bad hen, you! You pecked my hand so hard that you've made it bleed!'

Meddle collected all the twenty-four eggs into a big basket. The hens screeched and pecked at him, for they were upset to see

their precious eggs taken. But Meddle proudly took them back to Dame Henny.

'Look here!' he said, showing her the eggs. 'Twenty-four eggs you missed this morning! What do you think of that? It's a good thing I came.'

'Meddle!' said Dame Henny in amazement. 'Where in the world did you find them? Has one of the hens been laying away?'

'Oh no,' said Meddle. 'I found twelve eggs in one coop with a silly pecking hen on them, and twelve eggs in another.'

'Oh, you silly, stupid, meddling creature!'

cried Dame Henny in a rage. 'Those are the eggs that the two hens are hatching into chicks for me. You may have spoilt them! Give them to me! I must take them back at once.'

Dame Henny snatched the eggs away from Meddle and ran off to put them back into the coops. Meddle was cross. He went out and looked at the pigs.

'My! How hungry they are!' he said, as he watched them rooting about in their sty. 'I don't believe my sister gives them enough to eat.'

He rushed indoors. On the table was a big bowl full of some sort of mixture. Meddle took it and ran to the pigs.

'This must be meant for you,' he said, as he put the bowl down for the pigs to eat from. 'It looks like what they call pig-wash.'

The pigs ran to the big bowl and began to gobble up the mixture there with joy. Dame Henny came back from the coops and stared into the sty. When she saw her basin there she glared at Meddle.

'Where did you get that basin, and what's in it?' she asked.

'I don't exactly know what the mixture is,'

said Meddle. 'I found the bowl on your kitchen table, and as the pigs were hungry I though I'd better give them their dinner.'

'On my kitchen table!' shouted Dame Henny in a fine temper. 'Why, that was my mixing-bowl – and in it was my cake-mixture! There were eggs and flour and milk and currants and sugar in that bowl – and you've given it all to the greedy pigs! Oh, you wicked fellow! I'll box your ears for you, so I will!'

Meddle ran away and hid inside a shed. He didn't like his ears boxed. Dame Henny snorted angrily and went indoors. She had some buns baking in the oven and she didn't want them to be burnt.

Meddle looked round the dark shed. At first he thought he was alone, but then he saw a big animal at the far end.

'It's a cow!' said Meddle in surprise. 'Now why isn't the poor thing out in the field with the others? It must have been forgotten! Really, how careless people are! I will let the poor thing out into the air and sunshine.'

He went to where the big animal chewed quietly in its corner. It was tied with a heavy rope to its stall. Meddle undid the rope.

'Gee up!' he said, and the great creature lumbered out. It was pleased to be free and in the sunshine. It bellowed loudly.

'Gee up, I say!' said Meddle, and he swished the back legs of the animal with a twig. It bellowed again.

Dame Henny heard the bellowing and came running to the kitchen door. She gave a scream.

'Who's let out the bull?' she cried. 'Oh my, oh my, now what are we to do? Who's let out the bull? Help, help, the bull is loose!'

'Oh, is it a bull?' cried Meddle in alarm. 'I

thought it was just a cow. It was standing all alone in the dark shed and I thought somebody had forgotten it.'

The bull bellowed again and swished its long tail about. Its eyes gleamed fiercely as it looked at Meddle. It had not liked being hit with a stinging twig on its back legs.

'Meddle, you got that bull out – now you just take it back again!' cried Dame Henny.

'Well, it seems a harmless creature,' said Meddle. 'Bellows a bit, that's all! Hie, you bull! Go back to your shed! Do you hear? Pretending to be a lonely cow like that, and making me set you free! I never heard of such a thing! Go back to your shed at once!'

But the bull didn't mean to go back to the dark shed. It kicked up its heels and frisked round the farmyard, trying to find a way into the buttercup-field where the cows and the sheep grazed quietly.

Meddle was angry. 'Didn't you hear what I said, you bad creature?' he cried. 'I'll flick you with my switch! There! How do you like that?'

The bull felt the stick against his back legs and he didn't like it at all. He turned and glared at Meddle. Then he lowered his head and began to run towards Meddle.

'Run, Meddle, run! He'll toss you on his horns!' shouted Dame Henny.

'Stop, bull, stop!' called Meddle in alarm. 'I'll open the gate into the field for you. Stop! Don't be silly! I'm your friend!'

'Brrrrrrrrumph!' snorted the angry bull and rushed straight at Meddle. Meddle ran to the gate – but the bull caught him up. He tore two holes in Meddle's trousers and tossed him up into the air, right over the hedge – and, dear me, Meddle fell neatly on to a cow's back, smack!

The cow was in a fright when she felt Meddle on her back. She tore round the field with Meddle clinging to her horns – and at that moment Farmer Henny came back home from market.

When he saw Meddle on a cow he was very angry, for he thought that someone was having a joke with his cows. He waited till the cow threw Meddle off, and then he stepped up to him with his big stick.

'People that ride cows get a scolding!' he said.

'Oh! Oh! Stop!' cried Meddle. 'I'm Meddle, your wife's brother. Don't you know me?'

'Oh yes, I know you all right!' said the farmer, grinning. 'That's why I'm going to scold you!'

Meddle took to his heels and ran off like the wind. Farmer Henny laughed.

'I'll never visit you again!' shouted Meddle in a rage. 'Never, never, never!'

'That suits us all right!' cried the farmer, and he went to catch his bull.

As for Mister Meddle, he had to spend the next day in bed whilst Mrs Stitch mended his trousers!

Chapter 6

Mister Meddle Goes
to the Grocer's

One morning Mister Meddle took his shopping-basket and went to the grocer's. He wanted a dozen eggs. They were ten pence each, he knew, so he slipped one pound twenty into his pocket to pay for them.

When he got there, Mr Sugarman, the grocer, was not in his usual place behind the counter. He had gone out to his yard to get some oil for a customer. Mister Meddle wandered round the shop, looking at the biscuits and bacon and eggs.

Dame Flap came in and said good morning. She sat down on a chair and waited.

'I can't think what's happened to Mr Sugarman,' said Mister Meddle. 'I've been waiting quite a time.'

'It's a nuisance,' said Dame Flap. 'I'm in a hurry. I want some castor sugar to put on the top of a nice jam-sandwich.'

'Well, I'll get it for you,' said Mister Meddle, most obligingly. 'You can leave the money on the counter for Mr Sugarman when he comes in, and I'll tell him it's for a pound of sugar.'

He hunted about for castor sugar. At last he found a big tin-lined drawer of what he thought was sugar – but, you know, it was salt! Mister Meddle didn't think of tasting to make sure. No – he simply weighed out a pound, put it into Dame Flap's bag, and she put the money on the counter.

'It's nice to be useful,' thought Mister Meddle, sitting down to wait. As he waited, the doorbell rang and old Father Jenks came in.

'Hello, where's Mr Sugarman?' he asked. 'I want some caraway seeds. My wife is baking a seed-cake, and she's got no caraway seeds.'

'Let me serve you, Father Jenks!' said Mister Meddle, jumping up. 'I'll soon find the seeds for you!'

He hunted around, and came to a big tin of seeds. 'These must be caraway seeds,' said

Meddle, pleased. If only he had looked on the outside of the tin he would have seen that it was full of canary seed – but no, Mister Meddle didn't think of looking. He was quite sure it was full of caraway seeds.

He weighed out a little packet of them and gave them to Father Jenks. 'I don't know how much caraway seeds are, but if you leave fifty pence Mr Sugarman will send you the change,' said Mister Meddle grandly.

So Father Jenks put fifty pence on the counter, took up the packet, and went out. Mister Meddle really felt he was being remarkably useful. He hoped somebody else would come in – and sure enough, somebody did!

It was little Molly Miggle. She wanted some butter. Mister Meddle beamed at her.

He saw some yellow tablets on a shelf that looked to him just like butter. He took one down and wrapped it up. He didn't see that it was yellow soap. Silly old Meddle!

Molly Miggle put down sixty pence on the counter and went out. Mister Meddle was just going to sit down when Spink came in to do some shopping. Spink was a sharp little fellow who didn't like Meddle at all.

'What can I do for you this morning, Spink?' said Meddle.

'Do for me? What do you mean?' said Spink. 'You're not the grocer!'

'Oh, I'm just serving people till Mr Sugarman comes back,' said Meddle. 'Do tell me what you want.'

'Well, I shan't,' said Spink. 'I'm quite able to get what I want myself. I know you and your meddling ways.'

Mister Meddle felt angry. Spink walked over to the eggs and picked out one or two, weighing them in his hand to get the heaviest ones.

Meddle went and stood at his elbow. 'You are not to do that,' he said to Spink. 'It's not fair to take the best eggs. You should take them as they come.'

'Oh, go away,' said Spink, giving Meddle a sharp dig with his elbow. Meddle gave a squeal, and then dug *his* elbow into Spink. Spink shouted and turned on Meddle. He gave him a good shaking and then let go of him suddenly. Meddle fell straight into the box of new-laid eggs!

Crash! Smash! He broke about a hundred eggs at one go! He sat up in the box, covered

with yellow yolk, very angry indeed. Spink yelled with laughter and danced round the shop in delight. 'You can pay for them!' he shouted. 'You can pay for them!'

He ran out of the shop, still laughing. Meddle was just struggling to get out of the egg-box when Mr Sugarman the grocer came in. He stared at Meddle in the greatest astonishment. 'Are you trying to hatch those eggs?' he asked at last. 'I'm afraid it will be expensive, Mister Meddle.'

'Spink pushed me in,' said Meddle, trying to get out. 'You must make him pay for them, Mr Sugarman. I was only trying to stop him taking your nicest eggs. And I've been very helpful to you this morning, if only you knew it! I've served heaps of customers!'

And at that moment the three customers all came into the shop together, very angry indeed. Dame Flap slapped a blue bag down on the counter and glared at Meddle.

'You gave me salt instead of sugar!' she cried angrily. 'You muddler! You meddler! I've spoilt my sandwich! It's got salt all over it now instead of sugar!'

'And just look here – my wife says you gave me canary seed instead of caraway seed!' shouted Father Jenks in a rage. 'She emptied half of it into her cake mixture before she saw it was the wrong seed – and now I've got to spend the rest of the morning picking out those seeds! I've a good mind to pull your nose hard! Sticking it into other people's business like that!'

'And my mother says this is yellow soap, not butter,' said Molly Miggle, putting the soap on the counter. 'She tried to cut it to spread on our bread, and it wouldn't spread – and when she tasted a bit she found it was soap, and it made her feel ill. She's very

angry indeed.'

Mr Sugarman glared at Meddle. 'Can't you stop meddling with other people?' he said. 'I shall send you a bill for canary seed, soap, and salt, my dear Meddle. And I should like to know what *you* came to buy this morning? A pennyworth of sense, I should think.'

'I came to buy some eggs,' said Meddle, getting out of the egg-box, looking very hot and bothered to hear of all his mistakes.

'Well, you seem to have got your eggs all right,' said Dame Flap, giggling as she saw Meddle covered with yolks.

'Put a few into your basket,' said Mr Sugarman, and he shook the mess of broken eggs into Meddle's basket. 'I'll send the bill tomorrow. Good-day!'

Poor Meddle! He had to walk all the way home covered in egg-yolk, and he didn't like it at all.

'Have you sat down in a custard?' yelled the boys and girls he passed. Mister Meddle didn't say a word. He went indoors and put himself and his clothes into a nice hot bath.

And whilst he was steaming there, he made up his mind as usual that he wouldn't meddle any more.

Dear, dear! What a pity he can't do what
he says!

Chapter 7

Mister Meddle's Parcel

One day Mister Meddle went to get his shoes from the mender's. They were ready for him, so he paid the bill and took up the brown paper parcel.

Off he went, meaning to go straight home. But, of course, he didn't. He met Mr Jenks, who was sitting on the seat by the bus stop with a lot of other people, waiting for the bus.

So down sat Meddle and began to talk. Mr Jenks caught the next bus, and then, as Meddle didn't know any of the other people on the seat, he picked up the parcel beside him and set off home.

But he picked up the wrong parcel! He had put his parcel down on the left side of him – and the one he picked up was on the right side, and belonged to the big man there! But the big man didn't notice for a while. He just sat and smoked his pipe.

Meddle went on home, swinging his parcel by the string and singing a song at the top of his voice. But he hadn't gone very far when he heard someone shouting behind him.

He looked round. It was the big man, and he was shouting out very loudly: 'GIVE ME THAT PARCEL!'

'Good gracious!' said Meddle to himself, quite alarmed. 'What does he want my parcel for? He must be a robber!'

So Meddle began to run as fast as he could.

'STOP! STOP!' yelled the big man behind. 'I SAY STOP!'

'And I say go on!' panted Meddle to himself. 'Oh my, oh my! Who'd have thought of meeting robbers like this!'

He tore on and on. The man tore after him, getting angrier and angrier.

'GIVE ME THAT PARCEL!' yelled the man, who was really catching Meddle up now.

'Never, never!' shouted back Meddle

valiantly. He turned in at a gate, meaning to take a short cut across Farmer Straw's field. It was very muddy and wet. Soon poor Meddle had lumps of clay on his boots, and could hardly run at all. He staggered as he went – but the big man behind was in the same state!

He couldn't run either, for his boots had great lumps of clay all over them. But he made up for his slowness by his shouting.

'STOP, I SAY! STOP! I WANT THAT PARCEL!'

'Well, you won't get it then!' shouted back

poor Meddle. He stumbled over the field and at last came to the stream. This was usually so small that Meddle could jump over it quite easily. But today it was swollen and wide and deep, for there had been heavy rains. Meddle wished he hadn't got to jump – but there was nothing else to do!

So he jumped – but, of course, he landed right in the very middle of the stream! His parcel got very wet, and by the time he had waded out of the stream on to the other side, the paper was giving way. Meddle sat down on the bank, panting and puffing. He felt quite sure that the big man wouldn't try to jump, for he had seen what had happened to Meddle.

The man didn't jump. He stood on the other side of the stream and shouted once more to him: 'You SILLY! You've spoilt my parcel!'

Meddle thought the man must be quite mad. He held up the parcel, which was rapidly coming undone, and shouted back:

'It's *my* parcel! It's got my boots inside! You won't rob me of them if I can help it.'

The paper slid away, and big drops of water fell all over Meddle. He stared at the

wet paper – and he stared, and he stared!
For in the parcel were not the boots he had
expected – but a very nice large slab of
cheese that smelt exceedingly good – but was
quite spoilt by the water!

'Good gracious!' said Meddle. 'What's
happened to my boots?'

'You left them on the bus-stop seat, you
silly donkey,' said the big man impatiently.
'You took my cheese instead. And here I've
been shouting and running after you for
ages, and all you do is to yell back something

rude at me, jump into a stream, and spoil my cheese!'

'I'm really very sorry,' said Meddle in a small voice. 'Really very sorry indeed.'

'Well, being sorry won't mend my cheese,' said the big man. 'You'll have to pay for that.'

'Oh, certainly,' said Meddle. 'I quite see that. I'll send the money to you tomorrow.'

'Oh no, you won't,' said the big man firmly. 'You'll come across this stream again and you'll give me the money now. After all, you've got to go back to the seat to fetch your boots, haven't you? And you'd better hurry, too, in case somebody goes off with them!'

'Dear me, so I had,' said poor Meddle. So into the stream he had to jump once more. He waded across and paid the large man what he asked. Then, cramming the soaked cheese into his pocket, he set off back to the seat to get his boots.

The parcel was still there. Meddle undid it to make sure it really did hold boots this time, not cheese or something extraordinary. Yes – it was boots all right!

So home at last went Meddle, with a pair

of mended boots, a pocketful of dripping cheese – and no money!

And if I know anything of Meddle, he'll go to bed tonight, leaving the cheese in his pockets – and then he'll wonder why his bedroom is suddenly overrun with hundreds of mice!

Chapter 8

Mister Meddle and the Birds

One day when Mister Meddle passed by his Aunt Jemima's, he saw that she had some new yellow canaries and some little budgie-birds, too.

'Dear me!' said Meddle in delight. 'How pretty they are! I really must go and see them!'

He popped into his aunt's house, and she came running to send him out, for she knew Meddle's interfering ways.

'Now, Meddle, out you go!' she said. 'It's my washing morning and I can't have you around upsetting things and making muddles.'

'Aunt Jemima, I only came in to see your lovely new birds,' said Meddle crossly. 'Just let me look at them, now do!'

'Well, take one look and go!' said his aunt. Meddle peered into the big canary-cage. There were two fine canaries there, tweeting loudly. The budgies were flying free around the room, calling to one another. They had a little perch by the window and they often flew to this to look out and see the passers-by.

'Aunt Jemima, your birds haven't very much to eat,' said Meddle. 'Look – only just that bit of seed – and very nasty dry stuff it looks too! Why don't you feed them properly?'

'I do,' said his aunt, vexed. 'You don't know anything about birds, Meddle, so don't pretend you do!'

'Oh, Aunt Jemima, I know a *great deal*!' said Meddle. 'Birds eat worms and cater-pillars and flies and grubs – they love those. Look at that canary tweeting at me with its head on one side. It knows I understand it.'

'Well, you go and do a little understanding outside,' said his aunt, giving him a push. '*I* know somebody who gave fish-food to Sally Simple's canary – and gave her canary seed to goldfish. Ha, ha, that's all you know about birds.'

Meddle was really very angry indeed. He

walked outside in a huff without even saying good morning. But, as he went, he made up his mind to do something for his aunt's canaries and budgies.

'Poor things! Only that dry seed to eat!' he said. 'I'll collect some worms and caterpillars for them. If they were flying about like the thrushes and the blackbirds, that's what they would be feeding on! I'll take them to the birds when Aunt Jemima is out.'

So Meddle began to hunt about his garden for worms and caterpillars. He had a bag for the worms and a box for the caterpillars – and, dear me, what a lot he found! He found a few beetles too, and wondered if the birds would like those as well. He put them into a tin.

Then he waited for Tuesday afternoon when he knew Aunt Jemima went out to a sewing-meeting. He put all the things into his pocket and set off, thinking happily how pleased the birds would be to have a good meal. He crept into the kitchen of Aunt Jemima's house. Not a sound was to be heard.

'Good! She's gone already!' said Meddle, full of delight. He took out his bag of worms,

his box of caterpillars, and his tin of beetles.
He tiptoed into the front room.

The worms were very wriggly. Meddle
found it difficult to push them through the
bars of the cage. The poor worms didn't like
it at all. So Meddle decided to give them to
the budgies – but they were frightened of
him and wouldn't come for the worms. They
flew all over the room, perching on the
lamp, the pictures, and the curtains.

'Oh, very well, you silly things,' said
Meddle crossly. 'After I've taken all this

trouble you might at least be pleased to see me. Well, I'll hang the worms here and there and you can get them when you like.'

So Meddle draped the worms about the room – two or three on the lampshade, some on the top of the pictures, and one or two on the mantelpiece. Then he opened his box of caterpillars. They were very lively indeed.

'I'm not sure it wouldn't be a good idea to let the canaries out of their cage and give them a fly round the room,' said Meddle. 'After all, the budgies are loose. Then I can pop the caterpillars and grubs here and there, and all the birds can share them. It will be as much fun for them as flying round my garden to find them.'

It wasn't much fun for the caterpillars and worms! But Meddle didn't think of that. He put the caterpillars on the table and chairs and pictures, and he popped the beetles on the mantelpiece, where they immediately ran to hide themselves away.

The canaries were rather frightened when they were let out of their cage. They took no notice of the live food that Meddle had brought. The budgies didn't seem to want it either. Meddle was disgusted with them.

'Well, really, you might . . .' he began. And then he stopped and listened in a dreadful fright.

Aunt Jemima was coming in at the front door, and with her were five friends! This Tuesday was Aunt Jemima's turn for having the sewing-meeting at her own house.

Meddle got a terrible scare. There wasn't time for him to escape. He hurriedly squeezed himself between the sofa and the wall and hid there. He did hope that the six women would not come in that room.

But they did! In they trooped all chattering merrily, and sat down. They put their sewing-things on the table, and slipped their thimbles on to their fingers.

'Now, let me see, are we all here?' said Aunt Jemima. 'Sally Simple, Dame Grumps, Lucy Lettuce, Mother Mangle, and Fanny Fickle. Yes. Well, we can set to work at once.'

Now Sally Simple was sitting just underneath the lampshade, and on it Meddle had put two or three long red worms. He watched them from his hiding-place, hoping and hoping that they wouldn't wriggle off and fall on Sally.

Suddenly one long worm wriggled too far.

It fell off the silk lampshade right on to Sally's head. Sally gave a scream and put up her hand to find out what was in her hair. When she felt the long worm she squealed and squealed.

'Sally! Sally! What's the matter?' cried every one in a fright.

'A worm dropped on me!' screamed Sally.

'Nonsense! Nonsense!' said Aunt Jemima at once. 'How could a worm drop on you? Worms don't live in houses!'

A second worm dropped on Sally from the lampshade and she jumped up in fright. The third worm dropped on the table, and everybody jumped in horror.

'It *is* a worm!' said Mother Mangle. 'And, oh, save us all, what's that crawling on that picture?'

Everybody looked – and they saw a big and furry caterpillar crawling on the glass. Then Dame Grumps saw two beetles running along the mantelpiece, and she squealed loudly, for she was terribly afraid of beetles.

A fat caterpillar dropped on to Lucy Lettuce's hand, and she yelled for help. In half a minute every one was squealing and yelling, for they saw worms, beetles, and caterpillars everywhere. Then Aunt Jemima noticed her two frightened canaries hiding up on the top of the curtains. She hadn't noticed that they were out of their cage before, and she was very astonished.

'Jemima, this is a fine state for your room to be in for a sewing-meeting!' said Dame Grumps angrily. 'I'm going! You may think it's a funny joke, but I *don't*!' She gathered up her sewing-things and gave a scream – she had picked up a caterpillar too!

She jumped so much that she sent her silver thimble flying out of her hand. It dropped on Meddle, who was trembling behind the sofa. Sally Simple bent over the back of the sofa to pick up the thimble for Dame Grumps.

She saw Meddle's scared white face looking up at her, and she gave such a yell that Aunt Jemima dropped everything she was holding, and her scissors cut her foot.

'There's something behind the sofa!' yelled Sally.

'What is it? A worm? A beetle?' asked Lucy Lettuce. 'Really, this is beyond a joke!'

'It's some sort of horrid big insect with a white ugly face,' said Sally, and she sat down, plump, in a chair and fanned herself, feeling quite faint.

Well, in another moment Meddle was pulled out of his hiding-place, for as soon as Aunt Jemima spied him there she guessed all that had happened. She shook him till his teeth rattled.

'So *you* brought all these dreadful things into my house!' she said. 'Meddling again! Didn't I tell you that my birds like seed and nothing else? You take all your creatures home with you, Meddle, and don't you dare to show your face in my house again unless

you want a pail of cold water all over you!'

And she stuffed all the beetles, the caterpillars, and worms down poor Meddle's neck
and turned him out of doors. How he wriggled! How he shook! It was dreadful to feel

things wriggling and running all over him. One by one they fell out and ran or wriggled away, very glad to be free again. They had had a most unpleasant adventure – and, dear me, so had Meddle.

'I shan't try to do a good turn again,' he said in a huff.

Well – we shall see!

Chapter 9

Mister Meddle Goes Out to Stay

Once Mister Meddle went to stay with Jitters, his cousin. He packed his bag and set off in a happy mood. Jitters had a nice house and garden – it would be fun to stay with him.

But when he got there, he found that Jitters was cross. 'The fire is smoking,' said Jitters. 'I don't know how we are going to sit here and talk, Meddle. The smoke comes puffing out all the time and makes me choke.'

'Put the fire out and I'll see if I can brush the soot away from the back of the chimney,' said Meddle. 'When my chimney smokes I just get my little brush and sweep the soot from the back – just there – and usually it is quite all right again.'

'I don't think you'd better try to do that, Meddle,' said Jitters at once. He knew what happened when Meddle interfered with anything!

But Meddle took no notice. He got a can of water and threw it on the fire to make it go out. It sizzled loudly, and sent such clouds of black smoke into the room that poor Jitters had to run out at once, coughing and choking.

'Now,' said Meddle, taking up the brush that stood in the hearth, 'I'll just show Jitters

how clever I am at putting these little things right!'

He stuck the brush up the chimney and began to sweep. He swept a great deal of soot down on himself, but he didn't mind. After he had swept away all he could find, he put his head up the chimney to see if there was any more he could reach – and down came a whole pile right on to his hair!

My goodness, that made Meddle choke as if he had a hundred fish-bones stuck in his throat!

Jitters put his head in at the door and sighed when he saw the mess. 'Come out, Meddle,' he said. 'You've made quite enough mess for today. I'll get the sweep in now.'

Meddle was quite glad to leave the smoky, sooty room. He went into the drawing-room with Jitters and sat down in a chair. he leaned his head against a cushion.

Jitters saw the cushion turn black at once. He groaned. 'Meddle,' he said, 'Do you mind going upstairs and having a bath and washing your hair? You will make all my chair and cushions as black as can be. Do go, there's a good chap!'

Well, Meddle was always willing to do what any one wanted, so he got up at once. 'Certainly, Jitters,' he said. 'I'll do it at once. What shall I wash my hair with?'

'There's a tin of shampoo-powder on the bathroom shelf,' said Jitters. 'Mix it in a glass, and it will make a fine lather. You can use that for your hair. There is plenty of hot water in the tap.'

Meddle went upstairs, humming. It was rather fun to have a bath in the middle of the day. He turned on the taps. But unfortunately he was so long undressing that the bath overflowed on to the floor, and Meddle had to spend a long time wiping up the mess with a towel. It was a pity it was a nice clean towel, because it looked very dirty when he had finished!

Meddle got into the bath, which at once overflowed again. So he had to pull out the plug to let out some of the water – and, of course, he forgot to put it in again, so before he had sat in the bath two minutes, there was no water left!

'Oh, well, never mind!' said Meddle. 'I'm getting cleaner now. I'll do my hair next.'

He looked for the tin. There was one in a

cupboard, so he took it out. He emptied some of the white powder inside into a glass and ran some water into it. It fizzed up splendidly.

'A beautiful lather!' said Meddle, and he emptied it all over his hair.

But the lather soon went, and left his hair feeling very sticky indeed. Jitters put his head inside the door just then to find out how Meddle was getting on.

'All right, thank you,' said Meddle. 'But this shampoo-powder is rather funny, Jitters.'

Jitters took up the tin. 'This is a tin of my best sherbet-powder,' he said sharply. 'Do you usually wash your hair in sherbet, Meddle? What a sticky mess you'll be in!'

'Oh dear! I didn't look at the label,' groaned Meddle. 'Never mind – I'll soon get it right if you'll hand me the proper tin.'

Jitters gave him the tin of shampoo-powder and shut the door with a bang. He was getting a bit tired of Meddle.

Meddle washed his hair clean. There was no soot left. 'Well,' said Meddle, pleased, 'I really am getting very nice and clean now! I'll do my teeth too – my mouth feels very sooty.'

But Meddle couldn't find his tube of toothpaste when he looked in his bag. He had forgotten it. So he looked in Jitters' cupboards again, and there he found a half-used tube. 'Good!' said Meddle. 'I'm sure Jitters won't mind me using a little.'

He squeezed some out on to his toothbrush. It was a light-brown colour and smelt a bit funny. Meddle rubbed the brush on his teeth – round and about, and in and out. Then he set his teeth together and looked at them in the glass to see if they were clean.

'Nasty fishy taste this toothpaste has,' said Meddle to himself. 'And, oh dear – my teeth are all brown now! I wonder if my tongue is, too.'

He tried to open his teeth to look at his tongue, but, good gracious! he couldn't get them apart. They were stuck firmly together! In a panic Meddle picked up the tube he had used and looked to see what was printed on it. 'Best fish-glue,' he read. 'Will stick anything together – broken china, furniture, and so on.'

Meddle groaned. He went to Jitters in dismay and showed him the tube, pointing

to his teeth at the same time. Jitters laughed
and laughed and laughed.

'Meddle! What will you do next?' he cried.
'You wash your hair in sherbet, and you
clean your teeth with glue! Well, you won't
be able to eat or talk for a good while now,
till the glue wears off. You will be a very easy
visitor to have.'

But Meddle wouldn't stay. He was very
angry indeed to hear Jitters laughing. He
fetched his bag, put on his hat back to front,
and marched off to the bus.

But he couldn't ask for his ticket, so he had to walk all the way home. The glue wore off after a while, and Meddle could talk and eat; but he wouldn't eat fish for a long time after that because, he said, it tasted of glue!

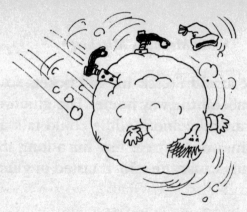

Chapter 10

Mister Meddle and the Snow

One morning when Mister Meddle got up he saw that it was snowing. Dear me, how it snowed! It snowed all night and it snowed all day.

'Just like great big goose-feathers coming down from the sky,' said Mister Meddle, as he watched the snowflakes falling.

He rattled the pennies in his pocket. Mister Meddle had four of them there – and that was all the money he had. It wouldn't buy very much. Somehow or other he must get some more.

'I think I'll go and see if any one wants their snow sweeping away,' said Mister Meddle. 'If I take my broom and my spade I might be able to earn quite a lot of money.'

So he found his broom and his spade, and put them over his shoulder. Then off he went to find some work.

He came to Dame Fanny's cottage. She was at the window, looking up at the snow. Meddle called to her: 'Shall I sweep a path to your front door for you, Dame Fanny?'

'No, thank you!' called back Dame Fanny. 'I don't trust you to do anything sensibly, Mister Meddle!'

Meddle was angry. Of course he could act sensibly! How rude of Dame Fanny! He would sweep a path just to show her how well he could work. So, as soon as the old dame had gone from the window, Mister Meddle set to work.

He couldn't seem to find the proper path, so he swept hard where he thought it was. After he had swept quite a long time Dame Fanny looked out of the window again – and, my goodness, how angry she was!

'You're sweeping across my beds!' she shouted. 'All my snowdrops were coming up there – and now you have swept all their heads off! Look at them there in the snow, you mischievous creature! Just wait till I come out to you!'

But Meddle didn't wait! He shot off down the road as fast as his feet would take him. 'How was I to know she was growing silly snowdrops all over the place!' he grumbled. 'Oh, I say! Look at that great pile of snow by the side of the road there! How dreadful! I will dig it away and sweep it flat.'

So he began. He dug his spade into the big heap of snow and threw it behind him. Then he swept it over the pavement, feeling very pleased to think that he had got rid of such a big heap of snow.

But he had hardly finished when Mister Biscuit the baker, outside whose shop the big heap of snow had stood, suddenly put his head out of his door.

'And what do you think *you* are doing?' he asked Mister Meddle, in a voice like ice.

'Oh, please, sir, I found a great heap of snow outside your shop, so I thought I'd better break it up and flatten it down on the pavement,' said Meddle. 'It was such a *big* heap of snow!'

'It was,' said Mister Biscuit, in a horrid sort of voice. 'I made it myself, Mister Meddle! I swept all the snow off my pavement, and packed it up into a big heap to melt – and now *you've* come along and undone all my work! The snow is all over my pavement again! Come here, you meddling, interfering little man!'

But Meddle didn't go to Mister Biscuit. No, he knew better than that! He skipped off down the road as if a dog was after him.

'I'm not really getting on very well,' said Mister Meddle sadly. 'Oh, look – what a lot of snow there is outside Father Flap's house. He's an old chap, so perhaps he would like someone to dig it away for him.'

So Meddle went up to the door through the thick snow and knocked on the knocker. Father Flap opened the door. 'What is it?' he growled.

'Father Flap, let me sweep away the snow from your garden,' said Meddle. 'I'm a good workman, I am. I'd be pleased to do it for twenty pence.'

'You're not a good workman, and I don't want it done!' said Father Flap. 'I like the snow there. It looks pretty.' He slammed his door shut.

Meddle sighed. He looked up at the roof and saw that the snow lay heavily there too. 'That's really very dangerous,' he said to himself. 'That snow will slide down and bury someone if Father Flap's not careful.'

Meddle opened the letter-box flap in the front door and shouted through it. 'Hie! Shall I make your roof safe for you? There's a lot of snow there!'

There was no answer. Father Flap had gone into his warm kitchen and shut the door. Meddle stood on the snowy step and looked up at the roof.

'Well, if I clear the snow from there, perhaps Father Flap will pay me for it,' he thought. 'If I make it all clean, and push the snow off, surely he will give me twenty pence.'

So he stood on the water-barrel nearby and climbed up on to the roof. He clung to a chimney and began to kick at the snow with his feet to clear it from the roof.

Now Father Flap was sitting snoozing in his kitchen with Dame Flap when they suddenly heard a most peculiar noise on their roof. Of course, they had no idea that Meddle was there! They both sat up and looked at one another.

'Cats on the roof again!' said Dame Flap angrily. 'Go and shoo them off, Flap; I will *not* have cats on my roof.'

So Father Flap went to the front door and opened it. He walked out on the doorstep and looked up at the roof – and at that very moment Meddle loosened a great sheet of snow with his foot and it slid down with a swooshing sound. It fell off the roof straight on to poor Father Flap underneath! It buried him from head to foot, and he began to yell and shout.

Meddle climbed down the water-barrel to see what all the noise was about. He was most astonished to hear shouts coming from the snow he had pushed off – but when he saw Father Flap's angry face suddenly looking out from the top, he guessed what had happened!

'Wait till I catch you, you meddlesome creature!' yelled Father Flap. He struggled out of the snow and ran at Meddle – but Meddle rushed away. Up the hill behind the cottage he went, up and up, hoping that Father Flap would soon be out of breath. But Father Flap was strong, and he was so angry that he meant to catch Meddle whatever happened, if he ran to the end of the world.

When Meddle got to the top of the hill he stopped. The other side was too steep to run down. Whatever was he to do? Father Flap decided that for him! He caught poor Meddle, gave him a good shaking, and then pushed him down the steep side of the hill!

Over went Meddle into the deep snow – but he didn't stop there! Dear me, no! He couldn't stop, because the hill was so steep – so down he rolled, covered with snow.

And the further he went, the more he was covered with snow, until at last he looked like a great snowball rolling down the hill!

Over and over he rolled, getting bigger every moment.

At the bottom of the hill some children were playing. When they saw the enormous snowball coming down on top of them they ran off with squeals and screams. The great snowball, with Meddle inside, rolled to the bottom of the hill, and came to a stop in the middle of the frozen pond. There it lay on the ice, quite still, with poor Meddle inside trying to shout and wriggle.

He couldn't get out, and Father Flap

wasn't going to run down the hill and help him, so nobody bothered at all. And there he stayed until the sun came out and began to melt the snowball.

Meddle was so pleased. Soon he would be free again – but dear me, the sun melted the ice on the pond too! And by the time that Meddle got out of the snowball the ice had turned to water, and there was Meddle splashing in the cold, half-frozen pond!

'Whatever do you want to go bathing in the pond *this* time of year for?' shouted the

village policeman. 'Come on out quickly, Mister Meddle!'

Meddle came out, wet and cold. He went home and got himself a hot-water bottle and a cup of hot milk. He shook his head sadly at his old black cat who was waiting for him to give her the skin off the top of the milk.

'It's no good trying to do anything for anybody,' said Meddle. 'Not a bit of good, Pusskins.'

Well, it all depends on how you set about it, doesn't it!

Chapter 11

Mister Meddle Goes
Out Shopping

When Meddle was staying with his friend Giggle in Heyho Village, he met all the people there and liked them very much. They didn't know his meddling ways, and they liked him too. So Meddle felt very happy indeed.

'If only I could help them and show them what a clever, kindly chap I am!' thought Meddle. 'At home nobody trusts me, and they all laugh at me. It's too bad.'

Well, his chance came very soon. It happened that Mrs Tilly, Mrs Binks, and Miss Tubby all wanted to go for a morning's outing together, and they couldn't.

'What should I do with my baby if I went out for the morning?' sighed Mrs Tilly.

'And who would do my shopping?' said Mrs Binks.

'And who would take my dog for a walk?' said Miss Tubby, who loved her little white dog very much.

Meddle was passing by, and he heard them talking. At once he swept off his hat, bowed low, and said, 'Dear ladies, let me help you. I can take the baby out in its pram, do Mrs Binks's shopping, and take the dog for a walk all at the same time! Pray let me do this for you!'

'Oh, thank you,' said Mrs Tilly, beaming at Mister Meddle. 'It *would* be kind of you to help us.'

She didn't know that Meddle loved meddling and that things always went wrong with him! She led him to where her baby lay asleep in its pram. It was a pretty, golden-haired child with fat little hands.

'There's little Peterkin,' she said. 'Now if you'll just keep an eye on him for me, he'll be all right.'

'And here's my shopping list,' said Mrs Binks, giving him a long list.

'Thank you,' said Meddle. He put the list into his pocket. 'And now let me have your dog,' he said to Miss Tubby.

Miss Tubby gave him her dog's lead. 'His name is Spot,' she said. 'Do you see his big black spot? He is such a darling little dog.'

The dog growled at Meddle. Meddle took the lead, and thought that the dog didn't sound a darling at all.

'Well, thank you, dear Mister Meddle,' said the three women, and they nodded at him and then went off for their morning's outing.

Meddle felt very proud. What a lot of help he was giving, to be sure!

'I'll walk down to the village now,' he said to himself. 'I can wheel the pram, and hold the dog's lead in my hand to make the dog come along too – and I will go to the grocer's and get all the things that Mrs Binks wants.'

So off he went, wheeling the pram, and dragging along the dog, who didn't seem to want to come a bit! Soon he met his friend, Mister Giggle, who stared in amazement.

'Whatever are you doing, Meddle?' he said. 'Where did you get that baby from – and the dog?'

'I'm helping people a bit, Giggle,' said Meddle. 'I'll be in to dinner all right. I've

just promised to mind this baby and this dog
and do a spot of shopping.'

Giggle began to laugh. Meddle looked
offended and walked off, pushing the pram
and dragging the dog. Soon he came to the
grocer's shop. He went inside, first putting
the pram against the shop window, and tying
the dog to a post. He pulled a list from his
pocket.

Silly old Meddle! It wasn't Mrs Binks's list
at all! It was a list he had made out for himself three weeks before – but Meddle didn't
think of that. He thought it was the right
one, of course.

He ordered all the things on the list. They were what he had ordered just before he gave a party. 'One pound of chocolate biscuits,' said Meddle. 'Two pounds of best butter. A two-pound pot of strawberry jam. One pound of shortbread, and two bottles of lemonade.'

That was all there was on the list. Meddle looked at it, feeling a little surprised. 'I thought it was a longer list,' he said. 'I must have been wrong about that.'

The grocer put all the things into Meddle's net-bag. Outside went Meddle, and walked to the first pram he saw. It wasn't Mrs Tilly's pram at all, nor her baby either! Somebody else had put their pram outside the shop since Meddle had put his, but dear old Meddle didn't think of that! He didn't even look at the baby inside. If he had he would have seen that it was a dark-haired little girl, not a golden-haired baby boy!

Meddle hung his bag on the pram-handle, put off the brake on the pram, and started for home. He hadn't gone very far when he remembered the dog! He had left it behind.

'Bother!' said Meddle. 'Oh, bother! Now I must go back to fetch it!'

So back he went, pushing the pram. 'Let me see, what was that dog like?' wondered Meddle, trying to remember. 'Oh yes – it was called Spot. It has a spot on its coat.'

He walked back to the grocer's, and when he was nearly there a large dog met him. 'Hello,' said Meddle, staring at him. 'You've got a spot on your back. You must be Spot!'

The dog wagged his tail. His name *was* Spot. Most dogs with spots on their back seem to be called Spot, and this dog was a very friendly one, willing to go to anyone who said his name.

'So you *are* Spot!' said Meddle. 'Where's your lead, you bad dog?'

'Woof, woof!' said the dog, gambolling round Meddle.

'You've lost that lead of yours, Spot,' said Meddle sternly. 'What do you suppose Miss Tubby will say to you?'

'Woof, woof!' said the dog again, not knowing at all who Miss Tubby was.

'Come here, sir,' said Meddle, and he caught the dog by the collar. He slipped a string through it and tied the dog to the pram-handle. Then off he went again. He took the baby for a long walk, and then went back to Mrs Tilly's garden to wait for her to return.

He sat there, reading, very pleased with himself. If only the people in his own village could see how folk here trusted him with their babies and dogs and shopping! Ha, they would be sorry they had ever laughed at him.

At twenty minutes to one Mrs Tilly, Mrs Binks, and Miss Tubby came back. They went into the garden and smiled at Meddle, who jumped up at once and bowed politely.

Mrs Tilly looked at the pram, and gave a jump. She went very red and stared at Meddle.

'Where's my baby?' she said.

'In the pram, of course, sweet little thing!' said Meddle, gazing fondly at the sleeping baby. He was a little astonished to see a dark one – surely the other had been fair?

'Meddle, this is *not* my baby!' said Mrs Tilly, looking fierce all of a sudden. 'And this is not my pram either, though it is dark-blue like mine. WHAT HAVE YOU DONE WITH MY BABY?'

She looked so very fierce that Meddle was frightened. He took a step backwards and fell over the dog. The dog growled.

'Be quiet, Spot,' said Meddle. 'How dare you trip me up?'

'*That's* not Spot,' said Miss Tubby. 'My dog is little and white with a black spot. This one is large and black with a white spot! WHAT HAVE YOU DONE WITH MY DOG?'

'Not your dog?' said Meddle, looking at the dog in surprise. 'Well, but he must be. How could a dog change like that? And how could a baby change either? You must have forgotten what your baby looked like, Mrs Tilly, and you must have forgotten your dog, Miss Tubby.'

'And what about my shopping?' said Mrs Binks, looking at the net-bag. 'Do you suppose that is what was on my list, Meddle?'

'Certainly,' said Meddle, opening the bag. 'Biscuits, lemonade, short-bread, butter . . .'

'I didn't put *any* of those on my list!' said Mrs Binks angrily. 'This is just a horrid joke you are playing on us, Meddle. Well, I won't pay you for those things – you can pay for them yourself, and take them home!'

Just then there was a scraping at the front gate and in came the right Spot, dragging his lead behind him! He had managed to get free! Miss Tubby ran to him and hugged him.

'So here you are!' she said. 'Did that wicked Meddle leave you behind, poor darling! You can bite him if you like, the horrid fellow!'

'Grrrrrrrrr!' said Spot, showing his teeth at poor Meddle. Meddle made up his mind to go – if only he could slip out without being noticed! But Spot wouldn't let him go. He stood by the gate, growling!

Suddenly someone came hurrying down the road with a dark-blue pram. She saw Mrs Tilly and called to her. 'Mrs Tilly! I've lost my baby! I found yours alone outside the grocer's shop, and I wondered if some one had taken mine instead. So I've brought yours for you – have you got mine?'

'Oh yes, I have!' cried Mrs Tilly joyfully. She rushed to her baby, and took it out of its pram, talking lovingly to it. Meddle thought it would be a good time to get out of the gate.

But just as he was going, Spot rushed at him and bit a big hole in his trousers! Mrs Binks picked a tomato from a nearby plant and threw it at him – splosh! – and Mrs Tilly called out that she would get a policeman because he had stolen someone else's baby!

Poor Meddle! He ran back to Mister Giggle's in a hurry. He fetched his bag. He wouldn't even stop to eat his dinner. He caught the first bus home – and went into his house with the biscuits, shortbread, lemonade, jam, and butter.

'I'm a most unlucky fellow,' he said sadly, as he spread butter on the biscuits, and poured out some lemonade. 'A most unlucky fellow!'

Chapter 12

Mister Meddle
Drives the Train

One day, when Mister Meddle was walking beside the railway line, he saw a train standing quite still beside a signal.

There was nobody inside the driving-cab of the engine. Nobody at all.

'Very peculiar,' said Meddle, looking at the empty cab in surprise. 'Most peculiar. I can't understand it.'

There were plenty of people *in* the train. 'All waiting to go on their journey, and nobody to drive them,' said Meddle. 'Dear, dear, whatever are things coming to?'

He walked across the lines to the train. He climbed into the cab of the engine and had a good look at everything there. He had always wanted to see the inside of an engine cab.

'I can't imagine why the driver and the stoker are not here,' said Meddle.

If he had only looked out on the other side he would have seen that the driver and stoker were busy picking the ripe blackberries that grew on the hedge there. They knew they had five minutes to wait before the signal went down, and they were having a nice time with the blackberries!

Well, you can guess what Meddle did! He touched this handle, and he pushed that one. He poked here and he poked there.

And suddenly he pulled a handle that started the engine! Oh, Meddle, Meddle, you are a dreadful fellow, really!

'Chuff-chuff-chuff!' The engine ran along the lines. The driver and the stoker jumped with surprise and dismay. They saw their train running away from them! They gave a shout and tore after it as fast as ever they could.

But they couldn't catch it. It went too fast. At first Meddle was frightened when the train began to go. He wondered if he should jump out – but when he saw how fast the hedges flew by, he didn't dare to jump.

'Perhaps I can stop the train,' he thought.

So he began to try all the different handles.

One let off the steam – 'Eeeeeeee-eee!' whistled the engine, and Meddle jumped so much at the sudden noise that he almost fell off the train.

The train rushed through a station. It usually stopped there, and the station master got the surprise of his life when he saw it rushing through. Whatever was happening?

Meddle pulled another handle. The train slowed down. 'Good,' said Meddle, 'now perhaps it will stop.' But it didn't, so he pulled the handle next to the stop-handle, and turned a wheel too, just for luck.

The engine began to puff very fast, and tore along as if something was chasing it! Oh dear, oh dear, it was a most terrifying ride!

People in the carriages began to put their heads out of the windows, wondering what in the world was happening to their train. They didn't like the way it behaved at all!

Meddle set the whistle going again by mistake. 'EeeeeeeeEEEEEE-EEE!' shrieked the train, and tore through another station.

Then it went into a long tunnel, and Meddle couldn't see a thing.

When the train came out into the sunshine again Meddle looked out through the cab window to see if there was another station coming. But to his great dismay he saw that he was coming to the end of the railway line!

'Oh, goodness!' said Meddle. 'Whatever am I to do? I don't know how to stop the train! It will bang right into the bumpers – crash!'

So he began to pull every handle he could see, and he turned every wheel this way and that. The poor engine didn't know what to do. How could it go slow and fast at once? How could it stop, and go full speed at the same time?

It began to rock like a rocking-horse, because Meddle had pulled down the handle for 'Go Backwards' and the one for 'Go Forwards' too. So the engine was trying to go forwards and backwards at the same time, and rocked like a boat in a stormy sea! It was dreadful.

It came to the buffers. It crashed through them. It leapt into the air, and then rushed forwards again – but not on the lines this time, because there were now no lines to run on. They stopped at the buffers.

The carriages caught against the buffers and broke away from the engine. The people all got out in a hurry, glad to be safe. They looked for their engine.

Dear me, whatever had happened to it? It had rushed over a field, and had come to the river. It had plunged straight into the water, and its big fire had gone out with a sizzling noise: 'S-s-s-s-s-s!'

And where was Meddle? He was sitting on top of the funnel, which was still puffing out hot smoke. He had been thrown there when the engine jumped into the river. It was a most uncomfortable place, because for one thing it was terribly hot, and for

another thing the smoke nearly choked him.

'Save me, save me!' cried Meddle. Some swans swam up in surprise. They were angry because this enormous puffing monster had dived into their river. They pecked Meddle hard, and he yelled: 'Don't! Don't! Oh, save me, some one, save me!'

A great crowd came on to the river bank. All the people talked at once. How were they to get the engine out of the river?

Just then a showman came by with two elephants, on his way to a circus. When he saw

what the trouble was he offered to let his elephants pull the engine out of the water. So
two ropes were fetched, and the elephants
pulled hard at their ends. The other ends of
the rope were fastened to the funnel by
Meddle.

With a jerk the engine came out of the
river, dripping wet. And just as it was hauled
safely up the bank, with Meddle still hanging
on to the funnel, up came the engine-driver
and the stoker! They had run all the way
after their beloved train!

'How dare you run away with our train?'
yelled the driver.

119

'I didn't know it was yours,' said Meddle. 'I didn't see you. I thought the engine-cab was quite empty.'

'You're a tiresome, meddlesome creature,' said the stoker. 'And you can just come back to the engine yard with us and clean our engine from top to bottom! It is all muddy and wet! That will keep you busy for quite a long time, dear Mister Meddle!'

Meddle hasn't been home for two weeks now. He is still busy cleaning that big engine. He hasn't done so much hard work for ages, and he has quite made up his mind that he will never, never drive an engine again!

Chapter 13

Mister Meddle
and the Clock

Once it happened that a bird began to make its nest inside the village hall clock. The clock always told the time to the people of the village, and it could easily be seen on the tower of the hall.

Meddle happened to be in the village hall when the bird's nest was seen. There was going to be a concert that night, and Meddle and some others were putting a great many chairs into rows ready for the night.

Every time that Meddle passed underneath the back of the clock, he heard a tweeting noise, and at last he looked up. A little bird sat there, holding a straw in its beak.

'Look at that!' said Meddle. 'There's a

bird building its nest inside the clock. Naughty, naughty!'

'Tweet!' said the bird, and that was all the notice it took of Meddle.

'What shall we do about it?' asked Mistress Fanny. 'It will stop the clock altogether if we let the bird build there. We had better get Mister Tock the clockmaker to come and see to it.'

'Oh, dear me, why bother to fetch Mister Tock!' said Meddle at once. '*I* could get that bird's nest out quite easily, and shoo the bird away too.'

'You'd better not meddle with it,' said Dame Flap. 'You always manage to get into mischief when you do, Meddle.'

Meddle pretended he hadn't heard what Dame Flap had said. He bustled about to find a ladder. But there wasn't one.

So he built up five chairs, all balanced on one another. They just reached below the clock. Meddle began to climb up. Good gracious! It did look dangerous.

'He thinks he's a clown at a circus or something,' whispered Dame Flap. 'I know he'll fall! Serve him right for meddling!'

Meddle reached the clock safely. He found

out where the bird got in and out. It was a tiny hole at the side of the clock's works. Meddle found the door that opened the back of the clock.

He opened the door, and looked inside. Dear, dear! The bird had built quite half its nest already! The clock would have stopped by the next night, Meddle was sure.

He began to clear out the straw, dead leaves, and moss. He didn't look at all where he was throwing it, of course, and it went all over the people below. They were very cross.

'Straw all over my hair!' said Dame Flap.

'Moss down my neck!' said Mistress Fanny. 'That tiresome Meddle!'

The little bird suddenly saw what Meddle was doing and flew at him in a rage. Meddle got a hard peck on his nose, and he was most annoyed. He nearly fell off the pile of chairs.

'Go away! Shoo! Shoo!' he shouted to the bird. But the bird wouldn't be shooed, and it flew again at Meddle. Meddle put up his hand to protect his eyes, and his sleeve caught in the works of the clock. He dragged his sleeve away, and as he did so he made the hands of the clock go round very quickly, so that they pointed to half-past twelve instead of to half-past eleven! Meddle didn't know that, of course – he couldn't see the clock face outside the hall.

The bird flew away, tweeting. Meddle tried to smack it as it went. He lost his balance – the chairs began to topple over – and down went Meddle and the chairs with a crash, smash, bang! Goodness, what a bump he got!

He picked himself up and dusted himself down. He was very angry indeed. He took

one look at the laughing people and then walked out of the hall in a huff.

And then, what a to-do there was in the village. The big clock was the one that nearly everyone used for the time. The people were always popping in and out of their houses to see what the time was by the clock.

'Good gracious! it's dinner-time and my pudding isn't made yet!' cried Mother Fiddle, and she hurried up so much that her dinner was quite spoilt.

'Look at the time!' cried Mister Gobby, as he hurried by. 'I'll never have time to get my dinner today before it's time to go back to work! What *has* happened to the morning?'

All the children were scolded for being late. They simply couldn't understand why the morning had seemed so short. They didn't guess that Mister Meddle had put the clock on a whole hour by mistake!

People had to wait ages for the bus that afternoon, because they were at the stopping-place a whole hour early. They scolded the bus driver, and he couldn't understand it at all!

'It can't be four o'clock,' he said, looking at the clock. 'Dear, dear, I thought it was only three. What a long time I have been getting here today. I'm very sorry, folks.'

The children all went to bed a whole hour early. The sun went down an hour too late, it seemed to every one! People were in a real muddle.

And then Mister Plod the policeman, who couldn't understand it either, had a good idea.

'The sun *can't* be wrong!' he said. 'I shall put on my radio and get the right time-signal.' So he did, and soon found that the village clock was a whole hour fast. Such a thing had never happened before!

'WHO has been fiddling with the village clock?' cried Mister Plod, in a great rage.

'Mister Meddle, of course,' said Dame Flap. 'He wouldn't let us fetch Mister Tock the clockmaker to put the bird's nest out of the works. He *would* do it himself.'

Well, Mister Tock was fetched to put the clock right. He had to get a ladder and put it up outside the village hall. He found it very difficult to put the clock right, for when Mister Meddle had caught his sleeve in the works, he had let a lot of straw drop down into the middle of the clock.

So Mister Tock had to look inside the clock as well as put the hands right outside. 'This will cost five pounds,' he told Mister Plod.

And who had to pay the bill? Yes, poor old Meddle, of course! Well, you really *would* think he'd give up interfering with things, wouldn't you? But I don't expect he ever will!

Merry Mister Meddle

Merry Mister Meddle

Enid Blyton
Illustrations by Diana Catchpole

BLOOMSBURY
CHILDREN'S
BOOKS

Contents

Chapter 1

Meddle and the Mice

'These tiresome mice!' said Meddle's Aunt Jemima, looking into the larder. 'They've been all over the place, look! Nibbling this, that and the other.'

'What about getting a cat, Aunt? asked Meddle. 'Wouldn't that be a good idea? She'd soon get rid of the mice for you.'

'You know I don't like cats,' said his aunt. 'Now, Meddle, I'm going out to tea, so please behave yourself till I come back again. I'll be back about eight, and we'll have supper then.'

Off she went. Meddle heaved a sigh of relief when she had gone. Aunt Jemima was always finding fault with him. It was nice to be able to sit down and put his feet up on the mantelpiece and read a book and eat as many peppermints as he liked.

As he sat there reading, he heard a scrabbling sound from the larder. Those mice again!

Meddle put down his book and thought.

'What about a mouse trap?' he said. 'I know where there is one – out in the shed. I'll get it and set it with a bit of bacon and a bit of cheese. I'll catch those mice for Aunt Jemima. Won't she be pleased?'

He went to fetch the trap. As he came out of the shed with it, the large black cat from next door came up to him and rubbed against his legs.

'Puss, Puss,' said Meddle and bent to stroke the cat. Then a bright idea came to him.

'Puss, would you like to sit in our larder and catch a few mice?' he asked. The cat purred. She went indoors with Meddle, and sat down by the fire to wash herself.

'I'll just set this trap, Puss,' said Meddle, 'and then you can go into the larder with it. What with you and the trap, the mice will have a very bad time!'

He went to the larder. He took the cheese from the dish and broke a bit off. He put it in

the trap. Then he unwrapped the bacon and cut a bit of fat from it. He put that on the hook too, and then carefully set the trap. He put it down on the floor.

'There!' he said. 'If that doesn't catch a mouse I'll be surprised!'

He forgot to put the lid back on the cheese-dish. He forgot to wrap the bacon up again. Meddle could never think of little things like that!

He called to the cat. 'Here, Puss! Come and watch for mice here. Come along.'

The cat didn't come. So Meddle went and fetched her and put her firmly down in the larder. Then he shut the door.

It was cold in the larder. The cat didn't like it. She didn't care about mice either, for she was well-fed and never bothered herself to catch them. She mewed and scratched at the door.

'You catch a few mice, and I'll let you out!' said Meddle, and put his feet up on the

mantelpiece again. The cat seemed to settle down and there was no sound of either mouse or cat from the larder.

Meddle made himself some tea after a bit and got the biscuit tin. He wasn't going to bother to cut himself bread and butter! He finished all the biscuits in the tin. Then he washed up his tea things, and went back to read again. But he fell fast asleep, and only woke up when he heard his Aunt Jemima coming in.

'Oh, dear, dear!' she said. 'I missed the bus, and it's half past eight and I'm so hungry. Why, Meddle, you haven't even set the supper! Lay the cloth, quickly.'

She stood before the mirror to take off her hat. Suddenly there came a loud noise from the larder.

'CRASH!'

'Whatever's that?' cried Aunt Jemima.

'Oh – I set a mouse trap there for you,' said Meddle. 'I expect that's the trap catching a mouse!'

'What – a crash like that!' cried his aunt. 'Oh, my goodness – there's another crash – and look, there's milk flowing out under the door! Mice indeed!'

She ran to the larder door and opened it. Out shot the big black cat; it jumped out of the window and disappeared. Aunt Jemima stared in horror at the larder.

'How did that cat get in here? Oh, my goodness, it's eaten the meat pie I left for supper – and the fish for breakfast – and it's gobbled up the custard I put ready – and it's upset the milk – and look at all this chewed bacon and nibbled cheese.' How *did* that cat get in here?'

Then she gave a scream. The mouse trap had gone off and nipped her toe. 'What's that? Oh, the mouse trap, Meddle, did you put that cheese and bacon in it?'

'Yes, Aunt,' said Meddle in a small voice.

'Well, why didn't you cover up the cheese-dish and wrap up the bacon?' asked his aunt. 'Didn't you know that even if the cat wasn't there to nibble them, the mice would climb up to the shelves and eat them? They wouldn't bother about the trap, if they could see cheese and bacon up here in plenty!'

'No, Aunt,' said Meddle, edging towards the kitchen door.

'Meddle, how did that cat get in here? Did *you* put it in?' said Aunt Jemima, suddenly.

'The larder window's closed. It couldn't possibly have got in by itself.'

'Well, Aunt Jemima – you see, Aunt – it's like this – after all, a cat does catch mice,' began Meddle. 'And I thought –'

'You thought it would be a very good idea to put that cat into my larder for hours, till it began to get really hungry and eat all our supper!' cried his aunt. 'Come here, Meddle, come here!'

But Meddle was gone! 'Good thing too!' said his aunt. 'There's only supper enough for one – an egg and bread and butter. Just wait till you come in, Meddle, just wait!'

Poor Meddle. He does his best, but it's such a bad best, isn't it?

Chapter 2

Meddle Does the Washing

Meddle was staying with his Aunt Jemima. He didn't like Mondays because it was his aunt's washing day then, and she groaned and grumbled all day long.

'Oh, how dirty you make your shirts, Meddle! Anyone would think you lived in a chimney, they're so black! And look at these hankies of yours! Have you used them to wipe up spilt ink or something?'

'Oh, dear – it's washing day again!' Meddle would think. 'I must really get out of Aunt's way. She grumbles all day long – goodness knows why! There doesn't seem to be anything much in washing. You just get hot water, make a fine lather of soap and get on

142

with it. I'm sure I could do it easily enough without any grumbling!'

He watched his aunt making the lather in the wash-tub. He liked all the bubbly, frothy lather. He dipped his fingers into it. It felt soft and silky.

'The better lather you have, the easier it is to wash the clothes,' said his aunt. 'But it's difficult to get a good, frothy lather these days. Get out of the way, Meddle. You'll have the tub over in a minute.'

Now the next Monday Meddle's aunt had a pain in her back. She sat in her armchair and groaned: 'Oh, dear, oh, dear! I can't do the washing today. I've such a pain in my back. I must do it tomorrow.'

Meddle looked at his aunt in alarm. 'Tomorrow! Oh, no, Aunt. You promised to take me to the fair.'

'Well, washing is more important than going to the fair,' said his aunt.

Meddle didn't think it was at all. He went into the scullery and looked at the pile of washing there. Horrible washing! Now he wouldn't be able to go to the fair!

Then an idea came into his mind. Why shouldn't *he* do the washing? It always looked very easy. And if he got a really fine lather it would be easier still.

'I'll go to Dame Know-all and ask her for a little growing-spell,' thought Meddle. 'I'll pop it into the wash-tub with the lather, and it will grow marvellously so that I can do all the washing in no time at all.'

He went off to Dame Know-all. She was out. Meddle looked round her little shop. Ah – there on a shelf was a bottle marked 'Growing-spells'. Just what he wanted!

He put fifty pence down on the counter, took down the bottle, unscrewed the lid and emptied a small growing-spell into his hand. It was like a tiny blue pea.

He put back the bottle and went out of the shop. He ran back to his aunt's in glee. Aha! It took a clever fellow like him to think how to make washing easy! What a fine soapy lather he could get. How all the dirt would roll out of the clothes when he popped them into the lather and squeezed them!

He peeped in at his aunt. She was still in her chair. She had fallen asleep. Meddle softly closed the door and went into the scullery.

He filled the wash-tub with boiling hot

water and popped in the soap flakes his aunt used. He swished them about with his hand, and a bubbly lather began to rise up in the tub.

Then Meddle put in the little blue growing-spell. It dissolved in the water and made it bluer than before. A little blue steam came up and mixed with the soapy lather.

And the lather began to grow!

Hundreds and hundreds of soapy bubbles began to form in the tub, and frothed out over the side, shining with all the colours of the rainbow.

'Good!' said Meddle, pleased, and he

stuffed all the dirty clothes into the frothing lather. He pushed them down into the hot water, and began to squeeze them. But he couldn't do that for long, because the lather had grown so much that it frothed right up to his face. Bubbles burst and his eyes began to smart. He blew the lather away from his cheeks.

But it went on growing! He had taken a far too powerful growing-spell from the bottle, and thousands and thousands of soapy bubbles were frothing up.

The lather fell out of the tub and went on growing. Soon Meddle was waist-deep in bubbles! He kicked at them.

'Stop growing! That's enough! How can I possibly do the washing when I can't get near the tub? Stop, I tell you!'

But the lather didn't stop. It crept along the floor frothing out beautifully. It grew higher. It sent bubbles all over the top of the table, and on to the gas stove. Gracious, what a sight!

Meddle began to feel alarmed. 'STOP!' he shouted. 'Are you deaf? STOP!'

But the bubbles went on growing by the hundred and frothed about everywhere.

Some of them rolled out of the window. The bubbly lather-stream went through the door into the kitchen. It frothed over the floor there, looking very peculiar indeed. Meddle began to get really frightened. He made his way out of the scullery, where the bubbles were now up to his neck, and found a broom. He attacked the lather with all his might, trying to sweep it back into the scullery, so that he could close the door on it.

But the more he swept, the quicker it grew! It was dreadful. Thank goodness the door into the sitting room was shut. Whatever would his aunt think if she saw a mass of froth creeping into the sitting room?

The larder door was open, and the lather went there, frothing all over the shelves. Oh, dear! It soon hid the meat pie and the cold pudding that Aunt Jemima had planned for dinner that day.

Aunt Jemima slept peacefully in the parlour. She had had a bad night and was glad to rest a little, with a cushion at her back. But when the noise of Meddle sweeping hard in the kitchen came to her ears, she awoke and sat up.

'What's that? What can Meddle be doing?

The kitchen doesn't want sweeping!' she said to herself. She looked at the shut door and wondered if she should call out to Meddle to stop.

And then she saw something very peculiar indeed. A little line of lather was creeping under the door! A little drip of lather was coming through the key-hole! Aunt Jemima started as if she couldn't believe her eyes. What was this strange thing creeping under the door? And whatever was coming through the key-hole? She wondered if she was still asleep and dreaming.

'Meddle,' she called, 'what are you doing?

Open the door. There's something peculiar happening.'

Meddle heard what his aunt said – but he certainly wasn't going to open the door and let all the bubbles into the sitting room! It was quite bad enough already in the kitchen. The froth was almost up to his shoulders. He couldn't even *see* his legs! Sometimes the bubbles went up his nose and made him sneeze and choke. His eyes smarted. He felt very upset.

Aunt Jemima watched the line of bubbles creeping under the door in alarm. As soon as the lather was properly in the sitting room it began to grow very quickly. It frothed up into the air, and Aunt Jemima got out of her chair in fright. What was all this?

She trod through the bubbles and opened the door into the kitchen. That was a terrible mistake! At once a great cloud of soapy bubbles swept over her, and she was almost smothered in them. She screamed.

'Meddle, what *is* this? What's happening? Good gracious, I can hardly see the top of your head!'

'Oh, Aunt, oh, Aunt, it's all because of a growing-spell I put into the wash-tub to make

149

a fine lather,' wept Meddle. 'It won't stop growing now. Oh, what are we to do?'

'Well! Of all the donkeys, you're the biggest, Meddle!' shouted his aunt, trying to make her way through the bubbles. 'Open the garden door! Sweep the lather into the garden. Don't let it fill the house!'

Meddle groped his way to the door, coughing and sneezing. He opened it. A great wave of froth immediately rolled out. More and more followed. It went down the garden path, and all the passers-by stood still in astonishment to see such a sight.

They had to get out of the way of the lather when it got to the hedge. It frothed over it and made its way down the road. Aunt Jemima watched it.

'Won't it ever stop?' said Meddle, really scared.

'It will stop when the growing-spell is worn out,' said his aunt, in a very grim voice.

The spell didn't wear itself out for four hours. By that time the lather had reached the village, and all the children were paddling about in the bubbles, having a lovely time. How they laughed and shouted!

But at last the froth grew smaller and

smaller. The bubbles burst and disappeared
and grew no more. By one o'clock there was
not a single bubble left. The wonderful lather
had gone.

Meddle was terribly hungry by this time. So
was his aunt. She went to the larder and
looked at the soapy meat pie and the cold
pudding. Then she went out to the hen-
house and found two newly laid eggs. She
brought them back and put them in a
saucepan on the stove to boil.

'You can have the pie and the pudding,'

she said to Meddle. But when he tried to eat them, he made a terrible face.

'Oooh! they taste of soap! Can I have an egg, Aunt?'

'There are only two, and I'm having them both,' said his aunt. 'Eat up the pie and the pudding.'

So poor Meddle had to, and they tasted far worse than any medicine he had ever had in his life.

'I shall have to do the washing tomorrow, just as I planned,' said his aunt. 'Next time you want to meddle in anything, Meddle, tell me before you start. It would save such a lot of trouble! As for the fair, don't dare to mention it! It might make me put you into the wash-tub with the dirty washing!'

Chapter 3

Meddle's Treacle Pudding

One day Meddle went to take his aunt some daffodils out of his garden. She wasn't feeling very pleased with him, and he thought it would be a good idea to make her a little present of flowers.

She was delighted. 'Well, there now, Meddle, if that isn't kind of you!' she said. 'You're a silly, meddlesome fellow most of the time, but not always. Stay and have dinner with me.'

'What are you having for dinner?' asked Meddle.

'Cold meat, baked potatoes, and a nice jam sponge pudding,' said his aunt.

'Couldn't you make it a treacle pudding instead?' begged Meddle. 'I do so like treacle puddings.'

'I would, if I'd got any treacle,' said Aunt Jemima. 'But I haven't. Not a drop! So you'll have to make do with a jam sponge pudding if you are going to stay and have dinner with me, Meddle.'

'All right,' said Meddle, and he picked up the morning paper to read whilst his aunt bustled round to do her work. But she didn't like that.

'Now, Meddle, don't you laze about,' she said. 'If you're going to spend the morning with me, you'll have to do something. I can't bear people who laze about.'

'Oh, dear,' said Meddle. 'Well, what do you want me to do?'

'I've got the workmen doing odd jobs in my scullery today,' said Aunt Jemima. 'You go and see if you can help them. Hammer in some nails, or something.'

Meddle wandered off into the scullery, but after he had hammered somebody's fingers, and upset all the tools into the wet sink, the workmen didn't want him any more. Nobody ever wanted Meddle for long!

One of them gave him a little pot with something yellow-brown at the bottom of it.

'Go and put this on the kitchen hob and stir it every now and again,' he said. 'That will keep you out of mischief.'

Meddle took the little pot. He put it on the hot kitchen hob. Then he looked round for something to stir with. He found an old spoon.

By the time he got back to the hob the yellow-brown stuff in the little pot was bubbling nicely. Meddle peered at it.

'My goodness me, if it isn't treacle!' he said. 'Look at that now! A pot full of melting treacle, and Aunt Jemima hasn't any at all.'

He stirred it. It wasn't treacle, of course, it

was glue. But that didn't enter Meddle's head at all. He was sure it was good rich treacle. He stirred it well.

'This would taste lovely on our pudding,' he thought. 'It's just what we want. I wonder if the workmen would mind if I had two big spoonfuls for our pudding. I'll ask them.'

So he popped his head into the scullery and called to them. 'I say, can I have some of this stuff on my pudding, men?'

The workmen thought he was trying to be funny. They laughed. 'Take what you like for your pudding!' called one. 'It's not what *we'd* choose – but if you like it, take it!'

Meddle was delighted. He went to tell his Aunt, but she had gone out shopping. She had left the pudding steaming on the stove. Meddle began to feel hungry. How lovely to have a nice sponge pudding with treacle all over it. Oooooh!

He laid the table. He got the dish ready for the pudding. He took the baked potatoes out of the oven, and wrapped them up in a napkin and put them into a dish to keep hot.

Aunt Jemima was pleased to see all he had done when she got home. She beamed at Meddle. 'Well, well – you *can* be useful when

you try. I'm pleased with you, Meddle. You
shall have two helpings of the pudding.'

Meddle didn't say anything about the
treacle. He thought he would give his aunt a
nice surprise. He left it simmering on the
hob.

Soon Meddle and his aunt were sitting
down to have their dinner. They ate their
cold meat, potatoes and pickles, and then
Aunt Jemima went to get the pudding. Soon
it was on its hot dish, and Aunt Jemima
carried it to the table. 'Now bless us all, if I

haven't forgotten to warm up the jam for the pudding!' she said.

'It's all right,' said Meddle. 'I've got some hot treacle for it! Sit down, Aunt, and I'll get it. It will be *such* a treat!'

He went to get it. He poured some of it out of the glue-pot into a sauceboat, and took it to the table. 'All thick and hot!' he said, and his mouth watered as he thought of the treat in store. He poured half of it over his aunt's pudding. He poured the rest over his own helping.

'It looks a bit peculiar,' said Aunt Jemima, doubtfully. 'And it smells funny, too.'

'It'll *taste* all right!' said Meddle. 'Try it, Aunt Jemima.'

They both took a big spoonful of their pudding, and then made two dreadful faces. Their teeth stuck together. They couldn't chew, they couldn't speak, they couldn't swallow!

Aunt Jemima stumbled to the bathroom to get some water. Meddle's eyes nearly fell out of his head with horror. 'It's glue!' he thought. 'It's glue! Oh, why did I meddle with it? Horrible, horrible, horrible!'

He couldn't say a word, and neither could

his aunt, even after she had drunk glass after glass of water. But she *did* a lot. She chased him round the room sixteen times. Then she chased him out of the house and up the road. Meddle raced away, large tears running down his sticky cheeks.

'Now, then, what's the matter?' said Mr Plod the policeman, meeting Meddle suddenly round a corner. 'What are you in such a hurry for? Just you stop and explain.'

But all that poor Meddle could say was 'Ooof-ooof-ooof!' so he had to go with Mr Plod, who thought he was being rude. And I'm very much afraid he'll have to stay at the police station till the glue is worn off!

Chapter 4

Mister Meddle's New Suit

'Oh, dear – I really do need a new suit!' said Mister Meddle one summer morning, as he looked at himself in the glass. 'My trousers are torn, my coat is dirty, and really I am surprised that my shirt holds together. As for my socks, they are nothing but holes!'

He went to look in his purse. There was five pence there, and that was all.

'Can't buy even a pair of socks with that,' said Mister Meddle. 'I've got to go to tea with Aunt Jemima this afternoon, too. Well, she'll just have to put up with my old clothes!'

He set off to go to tea with his aunt at about three o'clock. He had washed his hands and brushed his hair but he hadn't mended his trousers or darned the holes in his socks. That was much too much trouble.

It was a very windy day indeed. Mister Meddle wished he had a kite to fly. The boys and girls had all got out their kites and were having fun with them. The big windmill on the common was whizzing round and round. Mister Meddle's hat blew off three times, and he got cross.

He picked it up out of the dust and looked at it. 'Now you've got dirty, too!' he said. He brushed it hard with his hand and slapped it against himself. 'I do wish I had some nice clothes. I'm tired of looking like a tramp!'

He climbed over a stile to go across a field. He saw something peculiar flapping along the ground towards him and stared in astonishment.

'What is it? Good gracious! It's a shirt. A blue silk shirt! Now, whatever is it doing dancing about in this field all alone?'

He picked it up. It was exactly his size. 'This is a very strange thing,' said Meddle, and looked all round to see if by chance anyone had dropped the shirt. But there was no one about at all.

Then he saw something else coming

towards him. How strange! This time it was a pair of trousers! They were a bright red, and had stripes of blue running down the sides. Very, very unusual, thought Mister Meddle.

He picked up the trousers and tried them against himself. They seemed just his size. He felt very excited indeed.

'I do believe – yes, I do believe that my wish has come true!' he said to himself. 'I was saying how I wished I had some new clothes – and now here are some dancing across the field to me!'

Then he saw something else – something brightly red, like the trousers, with little blue buttons on the front. A coat! A really beautiful coat! Meddle could hardly believe his eyes.

'What a bit of luck! Here's a coat too. Yes, there's no doubt my wish has come true. And my goodness me, here come a pair of blue socks! I'll look about for some shoes, too – and a new hat would be nice.'

But he couldn't find either shoes or hat. Still, never mind – he had a wonderful set of new clothes, and he meant to put them on at once. So he went into a tumbledown cowshed nearby, took off his old clothes, and put on the new ones – the fine blue shirt, the red coat and trousers, and the blue socks. Lovely!

'I wish I could see myself,' thought Meddle. 'I must look awfully grand. What shall I do with my horrible old clothes? Here, goat, you can have them!'

A billy-goat had just put his head in at the shed door. Meddle threw him the clothes. The goat looked surprised. It sniffed at them, and then began to chew them up. It didn't

mind what it ate. Meddle's old clothes would make a very good meal indeed!

Meddle went joyfully out of the shed, dressed in blue and red. Whatever would Aunt Jemima say? She would hardly know him!

His aunt stared in surprise when she opened the door to him. 'Meddle! You've been spending far too much money on new clothes! You bad boy.'

'I haven't spent a penny,' said Meddle. 'Aunt, I wished for some new clothes, and they all came dancing up to me!'

'I don't believe a word of it!' said his aunt at once. Meddle looked very hurt.

'I'm telling the truth,' he said. 'They came dancing over the field right to my feet. Don't you think I look nice, Aunt? You're always saying I ought to have new clothes.'

'You look smarter than I've ever seen you,' said Aunt Jemima. 'Come along in to tea. There are some new ginger buns, and some lovely honey from my neighbour's bees. I hope you won't spill it down your new suit!'

Now, in the middle of tea, when Meddle was spreading new honey on his bread, there came a knock at the door. Aunt Jemima went

to open it. Meddle heard someone talking to his aunt in a very worried voice. It was Mrs Buzz, the bee-woman from next door.

'Whatever's the matter with her?' said Meddle to himself. 'Well, all I hope is that she keeps Aunt talking for a long time, then I can have lots of honey.'

He listened again – and then his hair stood up on his head in horror.

'My dear, I pegged them all out on my line, and when I went to take them in, they'd gone!' said Mrs Buzz's voice. 'Quite gone –

the blue shirt, the red trousers and coat, and even the blue socks. What Mr Buzz will say I really *don't* know. I suppose the strong wind blew them away.'

Meddle dropped a blob of honey on his coat; he got such a shock to hear all this that his hand trembled like a jelly. Oh, dear, oh, dear – so that's where his new clothes had come from – Mrs Buzz's clothes-line! Why hadn't he thought of that?

His Aunt Jemima came into the room, looking very stern indeed. Mrs Buzz was

behind her. She gave a scream when she saw Meddle.

'Oh! He's got all the lost clothes on! Oh, the rascal!'

'Meddle! How dare you take clothes off somebody's clothes-line?' said his aunt, in such a terrible voice that Meddle shook and shivered.

'I didn't. They danced over the field to me,' said poor Meddle, in a shaky voice.

'Take them off. Put on your old clothes and give these back to Mrs Buzz,' commanded his aunt.

'I c-c-can't,' said Meddle. 'I gave my old clothes to the billy-g-g-goat to eat!'

'You're a wicked fellow!' said Mrs Buzz. 'I'm off to get the policeman!'

She ran out of the room, and poor Meddle was terribly frightened. He jumped out of the window, and began to run home as fast as he could.

Just as he was getting over the stile, he saw a man coming towards him. As soon as he saw him, this man gave a loud shout, and rushed at the surprised Mister Meddle. He gave him such a blow that Meddle fell back over the stile again.

'You've got my clothes on!' shouted the man. It was Mr Buzz! 'How dare you! You give them to me at once!'

Meddle got up and raced away. Mr Buzz looked so fierce that he was afraid of him. Meddle rushed to the cowshed and disappeared inside. The goat was still there, chewing what looked like a heap of rags.

'Shoo, goat, shoo!' cried Meddle. The goat looked surprised, and backed away with a bit of Meddle's shirt hanging from its mouth. Meddle groaned.

'Is that all that's left of my shirt? And, oh dear, look at this coat – both sleeves have been eaten – and there's no sign of my socks – and you've eaten one leg of my trousers right up to the knee.'

The goat then heard Mr Buzz coming and moved to the door. It felt cross. Was someone else coming to disturb it at its meal? When Mr Buzz peered round the door the goat ran at him and butted him hard. He rolled over and over on the grass outside.

Meddle hurriedly took off his new clothes and put on his poor sleeveless coat and his half-eaten trousers. He couldn't put on a shirt or socks because they had been eaten. Then he went cautiously to the door.

The goat was having a fine game with poor Mr Buzz! It was dancing all round him, butting him whenever he tried to get up. Mr Buzz was getting angrier and angrier.

Meddle shouted to Mr Buzz: 'Look, here are your clothes! You can get them when the goat lets you!' He threw down the clothes and then raced off home, looking more like a tramp than ever, in his half-chewed, ragged coat and trousers.

He looked at himself in the glass when he got home. 'I can't go out like this! I'll have to

put on an overall and go to work somewhere, to earn money for new things. Just as I'm feeling lazy, too!'

He wondered if Mr and Mrs Buzz would come along with the policeman, and whether his aunt would come to scold him. Meddle thought it very likely indeed.

He found his overall, put it on, packed a little bag, and then went to catch a bus to the next town. He locked his door and put the key in his pocket.

'I'll get a job miles away!' he said, 'even if it means working hard and wearing an overall for weeks till I can buy a new suit.'

So, when Aunt Jemima came along to scold him she couldn't find him, and when Mr and Mrs Buzz came with a policeman he wasn't there.

Poor Meddle! He won't believe in wishes coming true again, will he?

Chapter 5

Meddle's Good Turns

Aunt Jemima was very cross with Meddle. He had been staying with her for a few days, and had managed to upset everybody, even the cat.

He had made the cook cross because he had gone into her larder at night and eaten all the jam tarts she had made for the next day's dinner. He had upset the gardener by borrowing his best spade and leaving it somewhere where it couldn't be found.

And he had upset the cat by treading three times on its tail in one day.

'You are very unkind, Meddle,' said his aunt.

'I'm *not*,' said Meddle. 'It's the cat that's untidy – leaving her tail about all over the

171

place for people to tread on. I believe she does it on purpose.'

Then he upset his aunt by telling her not to bother about watering her plants, he'd do it for her – and he took the wrong jug, and used up all the day's milk to water the plants.

'But couldn't you *see* it was milk when it came pouring out?' said his aunt, exasperated.

'I didn't look,' said Meddle. 'And if I *had* looked and seen it, I should just have thought your water was a funny colour, that's all. I took the jug you told me.'

'No, you didn't,' said his aunt in her very crossest voice. 'Meddle, I feel I'm going to shout at you very soon. Very, very soon. I can feel myself getting angrier and angrier. I can –'

Meddle backed away in alarm. 'I'm sorry, Aunt Jemima. Really, I am. I'm going out now so I shan't worry you any more this morning.'

'Well, Meddle, you'd better turn over a new leaf and try to help people instead of hindering them,' said his aunt. 'You go out, and when you come back you just tell me all the *good* things you've done. If you've any to tell I might not feel so angry towards you.'

Meddle put on his hat and went out in a hurry, treading on the cat's tail once more. The cat spat and dug its claws into his leg. Meddle howled, leapt into the air, and fell down the steps.

His aunt slammed the door and comforted the cat. The cook put her head into the hall.

'Has he gone?' she said. 'Ha, that's a pity. I've just discovered that a meat-pie is missing, and I've got a rolling-pin here to punish the thief.'

'He's gone,' said Aunt Jemima. 'He's going to turn over a new leaf, and do some good deeds for a change.'

'I'll believe that when I hear he's done some,' said the cook, and disappeared with the cat close behind her.

Meddle wandered down the street, a big hole in his sock where the cat had scratched him. He looked very solemn. He really and truly would do a good deed – if he could find one to do. There were always so many to do when he didn't want to – but now that he wanted to, it was difficult to find one.

He saw an old lady crossing the road with a basket full of goods. He ran to her at once, and tried to take away her basket meaning to carry it for her.

She screamed at the top of her voice. 'Help! Help! He's robbing me! Help!'

Then up ran two men and Mr Plod the policeman. 'What are you doing to this old lady?' demanded Mr Plod. 'Oh, it's you, Meddle, is it? What sort of silly trick are you up to now?'

'I was about to do a good turn,' said Meddle haughtily. 'Can't I carry an old lady's basket for her if I want to?'

And off he went, feeling very angry, his nose in the air. He was most annoyed. All that fuss, and he had only wanted to carry a basket for somebody!

He walked down a long street. A woman came out of a gate with a dustbin and dumped it down by her gate, almost on Meddle's toe. He jumped and glared.

'Sorry,' said the woman. 'It's dustbin day. We all have to put our dustbins out for the dustmen to empty.'

'Dear, dear!' said Meddle. 'Do you mean to say you have to drag out those heavy dustbins all by yourself? That *is* a shame!'

'Oh, I don't mind for myself, I'm strong,' said the woman. 'But I'm sorry for old Mrs Lacy, who lives down the road there. Poor old thing, she finds it a heavy job.'

The woman went indoors and Meddle went on down the street. He thought he would offer to take out Mrs Lacy's dustbins for her. That would really be a good turn to do.

There was only one house that had no dustbins outside. That must be Mrs Lacy's, thought Meddle. Poor old thing – she hadn't been able to carry them out herself, and nobody else had offered to do so for her.

Well, he, Meddle, would do everything necessary!

He went in at the back way and had a look round. My, my, there were three big dustbins there – no wonder the poor old thing couldn't lift them. Meddle knocked at the back door to tell Mrs Lacy he was going to take her heavy dustbins out for her.

'Blim, blam!' he knocked, and waited. But nobody came to the door. 'Must be deaf,' thought Meddle, and knocked again. 'Old ladies often are, poor things.'

But even his much louder knocking didn't

bring Mrs Lacy to the door. Meddle looked at the dustbins. He could quite well take them out into the roadway now, and tell Mrs Lacy when she at last came to the door. Or maybe she was out and he could tell her when she came back.

So, with much puffing and panting, Meddle got one of the dustbins on to his back and staggered with it to the road. He set it down with a bang. Gracious, it was heavy!

Back he went for the second one, which was even heavier, and dumped that beside the first one. He mopped his forehead and panted. This really was a good deed! He felt quite exhausted already.

'Only one more,' thought Meddle and went back for it. He soon had that one beside the others, and then he saw that he was only just in time, because the dust-cart was coming down the street already.

'Ha! Just at the right moment,' said Mister Meddle, pleased. 'I'll wait here till the dustmen have emptied the three bins belonging to Mrs Lacy, and then I'll take them all back again. She *will* be so pleased! If it hadn't been for me coming along just at this moment, she wouldn't have had them stood outside, or emptied, or taken back to their place!'

He waited till the dustmen came along. They lifted the first bin up and emptied it into the cart. A terrific cloud of dust went up and everyone sneezed.

Then the second one was emptied, and then the third. Meddle trotted back with the empty dustbins, feeling very good and virtuous. He wished his Aunt Jemima could see him now. She would be sorry she had thought so unkindly of him.

He stood the dustbins in their places and knocked at the back door again. The next-door neighbour heard him and popped her head over the fence.

'No good knocking. They're out,' she said.

'Oh, well, never mind,' said Meddle, giving the woman a sweet smile, much to her surprise. 'I only wanted to say I'd taken out the full dustbins, and brought them back again when they were emptied. Good day!'

And with another sweet smile Meddle went up the path to the front, and was gone. He ambled down the road feeling very pleased with himself. He thought he wouldn't mind doing another good turn. But what? He came

to a gateway. Beside it stood a pot of white
paint, and a brush stood in the pot. Nobody
was about.

'The man must have gone in to his dinner,'
thought Meddle looking at the gate. 'What
was he doing? Oh – repainting the name of
the house. Dear me, it so faint I can hardly
read it.'

He bent to see what it was. It really was very
faint indeed, and looked almost as if the
painter had tried to take away the name
before repainting it. Perhaps he wanted to do
it differently this time, with bigger letters,
thought Meddle.

179

'Fir Trees,' he read at last. He laughed. 'Well, well – isn't that just like some people! They call a house Fir Trees, and the only trees in the garden are rose bushes!'

He looked at the pot of paint. Wouldn't it be a very good turn if he painted the name again on the gate? The owner would be so pleased to come out from his dinner and find someone had done his work for him.

'I'm sure I could paint nicely,' thought Meddle picking up the paint-brush and looking at the white paint dripping off it on to the pavement below. 'It would be a nice job to do. Just the kind I like. Pity I haven't an overall or something, but I'll be careful not to mess my clothes.'

He began. He could just see the name 'Fir Trees' well enough to follow the letters over again with the white paint. He went over the line here and there, but he didn't notice that. He also dropped most of the paint on to the pavement and some on his coat and a good deal on his shoes, but he didn't notice that either.

'I'm doing another good deed,' said Meddle to himself. 'Really, Aunt Jemima has no right to scold me as she does. I can do more good deeds than she does. *She* would never have thought of taking out those dustbins, or of painting the name on this gate.'

Now, up the road, in the garden of the house whose dustbins Meddle had carried out to be emptied, quite a disturbance was going on. There was a lot of shouting and banging of dustbin lids, and the next-door neighbour popped her head over the fence to see whatever the matter was.

'Matter! Matter enough!' shouted a big, round, red-faced fellow with enormous black eyebrows. 'Someone's stolen the hen and pig food out of my bins! Look here – this is where the hen-feed was – and it's empty.' Bang! Down went a dustbin lid and another came up. 'And here's where the corn was and it's empty!' Bang! Down went that dustbin lid. 'And here's where the pig-food was, and it's empty!' Bang!

'Don't glare at me like that,' said the woman. '*I* haven't taken them. They've all been emptied into the dustman's cart.'

The red-faced man's eyebrows shot up till they almost disappeared. '*What*! Into the *dust-cart*! Say that again, Mrs Brown.'

She said it again, and then moved a little further away, afraid that her neighbour was going to burst with fury and rage.

'Who did that?' he spluttered at last. 'The dustmen? Did they dare to come and collect my dustbins? Why, they know I always burn my own rubbish and never want anything emptied!'

'No. It wasn't the dustmen,' said Mrs Brown. 'It was a funny-looking fellow with a long nose and untidy hair. He was banging at your back door to tell you he had taken out your bins to be emptied.'

The red-faced man could hardly believe this extraordinary tale. 'Where is this fellow?' he said at last.

'He went away,' said Mrs Brown. 'You might find him about the district if you go and look, though. You can't mistake his long nose – a real meddling nose it is, always being poked into somebody else's business, I should think.'

'It won't be poked into *mine* again,' said the red-faced man grimly, and he gritted his teeth together with a very nasty noise as he went to his front gate.

He walked down the road. Then he saw Meddle, who was still very busy painting the name on the gate. He had done as far as 'Fir Tre . .' and only had the letters *e* and *s* to do.

The red-faced man took a look at Meddle's long and pointed nose. Ha, there was no mistaking that! He tiptoed up behind him meaning to pounce on him unawares, but Meddle heard him gritting his teeth and looked round suddenly.

'GAAAAAAH!' yelled the man and flung himself on Meddle, who promptly sat down in the paint-pot and couldn't get out.

The brush flew up into the air and hit the

red-faced man over one eye. He stopped in surprise – and at that very moment out came the man who had been meaning to paint his gate and had gone in to his dinner.

He was very surprised to see one man sitting in his paint-pot and another man wiping white paint out of his eye.

'What's all this?' he cried angrily. 'Hey, get up out of my paint-pot, you! What are you doing here?'

'Sir,' said Meddle haughtily, trying to get up, but not being able to, 'sir, I was doing you a good turn. I was painting the name on your gate for you.'

The man looked at his gate and gave a howl of rage. 'What have you done that for? Fir Trees! You've gone and put "Fir Trees!"'

'Except for the last *e* and *s* I have,' said Meddle. 'That's what the name was, wasn't it? Though I must tell you I think it's a silly name because there are only rose bushes in your garden.'

'Well, what do you suppose I rubbed the name out for?' shouted the man. 'I was going to put "Rose-Cot" but I had to go in for my dinner. Now you've gone and put "Fir Trees" again. How dare you meddle? How dare you

interfere? You come along in and I'll douse
your head in cold water. I'll –'

'No, *I* want him,' said the red-faced man,
and put his heavy hand on poor Meddle's
shoulder. 'Do you know what he's done? He's
gone and let the dustmen empty all my bins
of hen-food and corn and pig-food into their
cart! Grrrrrrrrr!'

He growled like a dog and shook Meddle

so hard that he came off the paint-pot, and rolled into the road. Both the men pounced on him at once, but the red-faced man put his foot into the paint-pot and fell over. The other man fell on top of him, and Meddle scrambled up quickly to rush away.

How he ran! He puffed and he panted, and ran till he felt he would burst. He sank down on a seat at a bus stop and buried his face in his hanky.

'Oh, dear! Two good turns gone west! How was I to know the silly fellow kept his hen-food in his dustbins? I thought old Mrs Lacy lived there. And how am I to know if people suddenly change their silly minds about the names of their silly houses? Rose-Cot! Ooooh, what a name!'

Now, who should come by to catch the next bus just then but his Aunt Jemima. Meddle saw her and moved up to give her room. He forgot that he had been sitting in a pot of white paint, and he had covered the seat with white patches. Before she could stop herself Aunt Jemima had sat down on a patch of wet paint. She leapt up again with a cry and craned her head over her back.

'Oh! My best black velvet skirt! You did that

on purpose, Meddle! You wicked fellow! Now you just come along home with me, and I'll show you what happens to people who put white paint on seats for me to sit on. A good scolding is what you need!'

Poor Meddle – if only he didn't meddle in other people's affairs he would get on much better, wouldn't he?

Chapter 6

Meddle in a Fog

'I'm going out to buy some sweets, Aunt Jemima,' said Meddle. 'Do you want any letters posted?'

'No, I don't. And you're not going out in this fog, Meddle,' said his aunt, firmly.

'What fog? Dear me, I hadn't noticed that it was foggy,' said Meddle, looking out of the window in surprise.

'No. You never notice things like that, unless it's pointed out to you,' said his aunt. 'The times you go out in the rain without your umbrella! The times you –'

Meddle scowled. If Aunt Jemima was going to scold him all afternoon he didn't want to stay in! Anyway, the fog wasn't very thick. It wouldn't in the least matter going out in it.

He got up. 'The fog's not too thick,' he said. 'I think I'll just go out and get my sweets, Aunt Jemima.'

'No. Sit down,' said his aunt. 'You know that old Mrs Trottle may be coming to tea this afternoon if it isn't too foggy – and I want you to change into your clean suit, and wash your dirty hands and brush your hair. Otherwise you certainly can't come and have tea with us – and that means you won't have any cake or jam sandwich.'

'Oooh – is there to be a special tea?' said Meddle, who was greedy. 'All right, I'll go and change now, and get as clean as I can.'

But he didn't go upstairs to change. He tip-toed to the back door and let himself out! 'I'm going to get my sweets, whatever mean old Aunt Jemima says!' he thought. '*I* shan't get lost in the fog! Aunt will never know, because she will think I am upstairs changing my clothes and washing myself!'

And out into the fog he went. It wasn't too bad, really. He could see about three yards in front of him, and he made his way to the sweet shop quite easily. He bought his sweets and then went to look round the pet shop next door. It was a good thing he had no more money to spend or he would have bought a black dog, a white cat, two mice and a parrot that would say 'Pass the salt, please,' and then cackle loudly just like a hen that has laid an egg. Meddle thought it was wonderful.

When he got out of the pet shop the fog was much thicker. Oh, dear – he could hardly see his way at all now! He groped down the street, feeling the railings at one side.

He got to the corner and went round it. Then he wondered if it was the wrong corner. He looked at the names on the gates. Oh, dear – he didn't know them at all!

'Cosy-Cot! Why, that's not a house near us,' he said to himself! 'And here's Green Gates – I never remember seeing that in my life! I'd better go back to the corner.'

So he did, and crossed the road there and went over to the other side. 'This must be right now,' he thought. 'Now – down this road, round the corner, turn to the left, and there I shall be, at home! I shall creep in at the back door, go upstairs to wash and change – and Aunt Jemima will never, never know I've been out. Wouldn't I get a scolding if she did!'

But he didn't come to his aunt's house. He stopped in despair. 'I must be lost! This fog's so thick, now, I can hardly see. And it's getting dark, too. Bother! What shall I do?'

He went a little further on, hoping to meet someone and ask the way. But he didn't meet anyone at all. He stood still and frowned.

Was he anywhere near his home at all? He *must* find it because if he didn't Aunt Jemima would send out a search party for him, and would be so cross when he was found and brought back. Besides he would miss that lovely tea if he wasn't quick!

He thought of the tea. Chocolate cake with cream in the middle – jam sandwich that melted in his mouth – and perhaps some of those shortbread biscuits that Aunt Jemima made so well. He set off walking again.

But still he couldn't find out where he was. And now it really was getting darker. 'I'll have to go in at a gate, knock on a front door, and ask how to get to my own home,' thought Meddle at last. So he went in at the nearest gate, marched up the path and banged on the front door.

Footsteps came down the hall, which was

dark. The door opened and someone peered out.

'Please,' said Meddle, 'I'm lost in the fog. I want to get home quickly because my aunt is having a very nice tea – so could you tell me where I live?'

'Yes,' said the person at the door, 'you live here!'

And Meddle was dragged indoors and the door was slammed shut. It was his Aunt Jemima speaking to him! He had chosen his very own house to come and ask at for help! Well, well, well – how exactly like poor old Meddle!

'Oh, Aunt Jemima – oh dear – you see I just slipped out for a minute, and . . .' stammered Meddle, but after giving him a very hard stare, Aunt Jemima disappeared into the sitting room and shut the door. Meddle heard the sound of voices.

He remembered the lovely tea. He shot upstairs. He was very dirty and untidy. It took him a long time to get himself clean, brush his hair down well, and change into his other clothes.

'Now I'll go down,' he said, looking at himself in the glass. 'I look very neat and nice. I can hear Mrs Trottle is still downstairs – Aunt won't say anything nasty to me in front of her, and I'll soon tuck into the cakes.'

So down he went, practising a polite party smile, as he trotted down the stairs. He opened the door and walked in, bowing politely to old Mrs Trottle, and asking her how she was.

'Oh – there you are at last, Meddle,' said his aunt. 'Well, all the tea-things are stacked up in the kitchen, ready for you to wash. You can go and do them now!'

Well, well, well – what a shock for Meddle. He found himself out in the cold kitchen, faced by an enormous pile of dirty cups and saucers and knives and spoons and plates and dishes! He scowled.

'I'll jolly well tuck into the cakes first,' he said. But he couldn't! Aunt Jemima had put them away and locked the cupboard door.

And will you believe it, when he had washed up and went upstairs gloomily to fetch his sweets to eat, his aunt's old dog had been there first! Not a sweet was left in the bag.

But Aunt Jemima wouldn't scold the dog. 'All these things have happened because you were stupid and disobedient, Meddle,' she said. 'In fact, the only clever thing you did was to pick your own house to come to when you were lost.'

'It wasn't clever,' said poor Meddle, feeling very miserable indeed. 'It was just about the silliest thing I could have done. And if ever I lose myself in a fog again I'll be jolly careful I don't get lost exactly outside my own house!'

Chapter 7

Meddle and the Biggle-Gobble

'Meddle, for goodness' sake, go out for a walk and stop meddling in my cooking,' said Aunt Jemima, crossly. 'You've put salt in the pie instead of sugar, and dropped all the currants on the floor, and –'

'All right, Aunt, all right. No need to get cross just because I'm helping,' said Meddle, and he reached for his hat. He had just spilt the custard powder, and he thought he had better go out before his aunt discovered that, too. Dear, dear – what a pity people wouldn't let him be kind and help them more!

Meddle had one of his interfering moods on when he felt he could do things very much better than anyone else. He wondered if he should call at the butcher's and tell him how to make bigger sausages. He decided he wouldn't because the butcher had a nasty-looking chopper and might chase him.

'I might, perhaps, go in and tell the baker how to make a much, much richer fruit cake by putting in twice as many raisins and currants,' he said, but when he peeped in at the baker's shop window he saw that Mrs Biscuit, the baker's wife, was at the counter that day, instead of the kindly baker himself.

'She's quite likely to throw hard, stale buns at me if I try to help her,' thought Meddle. 'And, what's more, she'd probably hit me every time. No – I won't help the baker today.'

He walked on till he came to Dame Rimminy's cottage. He saw green smoke coming from her chimney, so he knew she was making spells that morning. Ah, now – if he could help *her*, how grateful she would be! He walked up to the door.

It was wide open. Meddle looked inside. There was a small round room, and in the middle of it was a peculiar fire with green flames. On it hung a black pot out of which green smoke came. Dame Rimminy was making a really fine spell, no doubt about that!

Meddle looked for her. She wasn't there. She was at the bottom of her garden looking for the very earliest snowdrop, which she wanted for her spell.

Meddle tiptoed to the pot. My, my – how it gurgled and bubbled! What spell was Dame Rimminy making?

He caught sight of a big, black book on a nearby table – 'The Big Book of Useful Spells'. Meddle read its title and then looked at the page where the book was opened.

'Ha – A Spell for Making a Biggle-Gobble,' he read out loud. 'Dear me – a *Biggle-Gobble*. What *can* that be? I've never heard of such a thing before. How very, very exciting!'

He read the directions: 'Get the pot boiling till the smoke is green. Now put in one cat's hair, half a spoonful of rice dipped in red ink, one old shoe, two pinches of Glory Powder, and stir with a feathered hat. Chant the following three times, and then wait five minutes for the Biggle-Gobble to appear.'

Meddle smiled happily. Why – he could do all that easily! Perhaps if he made the Biggle-Gobble, whatever it was, for Dame Rimminy, she would be so pleased with him that she would give him one of her famous Magic Toffees. You put one in your mouth, and, however much you sucked it, you could never, never suck it all away. Meddle had always longed for a Magic Toffee.

He began to make the spell. 'One cat's hair. Come here, Puss. Now, keep still, I only want *one* hair. I'm going to pull. Oh, you naughty cat, you scratched me!'

So she had – but Meddle had some hairs. He dropped one into the pot. Then he found a tin labelled '*Rice*' and took out half a spoonful. He found the bottle of red ink in Dame Rimminy's desk, and poured it over the rice. It went bright red immediately.

'Into the pot with you!' said Meddle, and into the pot went the rice dyed red! The pot gave a sudden gurgle and made Meddle jump. He peered into it. Was the Biggle-Gobble forming already?

'Now to put in one old shoe,' he said, and he looked for one. He saw two shoes belonging to Dame Rimminy standing on the floor. He looked at them. 'Well – they're not new, so I suppose they might be called *old*,' he said.

He picked one up and flung it into the bubbling pot. It almost bubbled over, and a strange snorting noise began to come out of it. Meddle felt rather alarmed. Still – he must certainly go on with the spell now. It was very, very bad to begin a spell and not to finish it.

'Now for two pinches of Glory-Powder,' said Meddle, and looked all round for it. Ah – there it was, in a tin on the top shelf. He climbed up and got it. He scattered two pinches of the curious yellow powder into the pot.

It jerked and bubbled and snorted as if

something alive was in it. Meddle felt quite excited. 'Now I must stir it with a feathered hat and chant the magic words!' he said.

He looked about and saw a fine feathered hat belonging to Dame Rimminy hanging on a peg. Ah! – that was just the thing.

He took it and began to stir the bubbling pot with it, chanting the magic words: 'Chirimmy, chuckadee, lillity-loo, Come Biggle-Gobble, I'm waiting for you. Chirimmy, chuckadee, lillity-loo!'

He threw the wet-feathered hat on the floor and waited. Five minutes more and the Biggle-Gobble would appear! Whatever would it be like? Wouldn't Dame Rimminy be pleased to see that he had made the spell for her!

But at that very moment Dame Rimminy came in with a small snowdrop. She glared at Meddle.

'What are *you* here for? You know I don't like anyone here when I'm making a spell. Get out!'

'Oh, but Dame Rimminy – I've been saving you a lot of trouble,' said Meddle, smiling. '*I've* made your spell for you. It will soon be ready!'

'Nonsense!' said Dame Rimminy. 'No one can make a Flyaway Spell except me!'

'A – a *Flyaway* Spell, did you say?' said Meddle, puzzled. 'But – but I thought you were making a Biggle-Gobble spell!'

'Don't be silly. Who wants a Biggle-Gobble?' said Dame Rimminy.

'Your book was open at that spell,' said poor Meddle. Dame Rimminy stepped over to it. She turned over the page and showed Meddle what was printed there, 'How to Make a Flyaway Spell.'

'The wind blew the page over, that's all,' she said. 'I wasn't going to make a Biggle-Gobble spell. Whatever *would* I do with a hungry Biggle-Gobble!'

'Are they hungry?' said Meddle, edging towards the door, and watching the bubbling pot with great alarm.

'Always hungry,' said Dame Rimminy. Then she caught sight of her feathered hat lying in a puddle on the floor. She pounced on it.

'Meddle! MEDDLE! You haven't been using my best hat to stir the pot with, have you? And where is my other shoe? Have you thrown that in the pot? Come here, Meddle. Stand still and answer me or I'll

scold you from now until tomorrow. Come *here*, Meddle!'

But Meddle was tearing round and round the room, trying to get away from the angry old dame. And all the time the pot kept bubbling and gurgling and snorting. Three minutes had gone – four minutes – FIVE MINUTES!

BANG! CRASH! SNORT!

Out of the pot leapt a Biggle-Gobble. Meddle stared at it in the greatest alarm. It was rather like a small dragon, with a round head like a cat's, and long ears – and far, far too many teeth! It stood and snorted in the middle of the floor.

'After him, Biggle-Gobble!' shouted Dame Rimminy. 'After him! If you're hungry, he's the one to catch!'

Meddle gave a loud yell and leapt straight out of the window. The Biggle-Gobble leapt out too. And then, my word, what a wonderful chase there was! Down the garden and over the wall, along the street and round the corner, over the stile and across the field,

into the lane and up the hill, along the High Street and helter-skelter for Meddle's Aunt Jemima!

The Biggle-Gobble thoroughly enjoyed it. But Meddle didn't. His heart beat so fast and he panted so loudly that he really frightened himself. Why, oh, why, had he meddled in that spell, and made a Biggle-Gobble!

He rushed into his aunt's house – but before he could bang on the door the Biggle-Gobble was in the hall too. Aunt Jemima heard the noise and came out of the kitchen in surprise. When she saw the Biggle-Gobble she gave a shriek.

'A Biggle-Gobble! How *dare* you bring one home, Meddle! It'll eat everything! They're always hungry!'

'Don't let it eat me, don't let it,' wailed Meddle, and dived behind the sofa.

'Where did it come from?' demanded Aunt Jemima, flapping at the Biggle-Gobble with a newspaper, just as if it were a wasp.

'From Dame Rimminy's,' sobbed poor Meddle.

'I'll telephone her at once and tell her to come and take it away,' said Aunt Jemima. 'Oh, my goodness, it's eating up all my new cakes. Shoo, you greedy creature, shoo!'

She went to the telephone and rang up Dame Rimminy. 'What do you want to go making Biggle-Gobbles for? One has chased Meddle home and it's eating my cakes. *What's* that you say? *Meddle* made it? It's his Biggle-Gobble, and he can keep it? But, I tell you, it's in my house and won't go away. I *won't* keep it!'

She slammed down the telephone receiver and glared at the Biggle-Gobble, who was now eating a pie. 'Stop that!' she shouted. 'Go and nibble Meddle's toes. Go and nibble his red ears.'

'No, no, Aunt,' wailed Meddle, and fled out of the door in fright. The Biggle-Gobble followed him at once. Aunt Jemima shut the door with a bang and bolted it. Then she fastened all the windows. Meddle could play about with the Biggle-Gobble all he liked – it wasn't coming back *here*!

The Biggle-Gobble gave Meddle a nip with its sharp teeth, but it didn't like the taste of him. So it trotted off to somebody's dustbin, took the lid off and began to gobble up potato peel. Meddle slid round the corner and ran off at top speed.

He went back to his aunt's at sixty miles an hour, climbed up the tree outside his window, and broke the glass to get in. His Aunt Jemima was very angry, and chased him up and down stairs just like the Biggle-Gobble – except that she had a very nasty walking stick in her hand.

Poor Meddle. He's afraid to go out of the house in case he meets the Biggle-Gobble, so he's got to stay indoors and scrub and wash and polish till his arms are ready to drop off.

'I'll never meddle with spells again,' he says. 'That awful Biggle-Gobble! I do hope it isn't still waiting for me round the corner.'

It isn't. It went back to Dame Rimminy and she gave it a good meal of dog biscuits and milk, and it curled up by the fire and went to sleep, purring. She sold it to the Green Witch for three golden pounds, because the witch had too many mice and the Biggle-Gobble was really a wonderful mouser.

But, Meddle doesn't know that. He thinks it's still looking for him!

Chapter 8

Meddle Goes Shopping

One day Meddle went to see his Aunt Jemima. He had been keeping away from her for some time because she wasn't at all pleased with his meddling ways.

He found a note on the back door.

'Baker. One loaf, please.'

'Milkman. One pint, please.'

'Laundry. Look in scullery.'

'Dear me!' thought Meddle. 'Aunt Jemima must be out, or else she's ill in bed. I'll go in and see.'

So he pushed open the kitchen door and in he went. No one seemed to be about. Meddle went to the larder door and opened it. Ooooh! Jam tarts on a plate. He was just about to take one when a voice made him jump.

'If that's the baker, leave a cake, too!'

'It isn't the baker. It's me, Meddle,' called Meddle. 'Where are you, Aunt Jemima?'

'I've got a chill and I'm in bed,' said the voice, rather croakily. 'Come up and see me. And DON'T snoop round the larder, Meddle. I know exactly how many jam tarts there are.'

Meddle frowned, shut the larder door softly, and went upstairs. His aunt was in bed with an enormous night-cap on, and a great array of medicine bottles by her side.

'Poor Aunt Jemima! Can I do anything for you?' asked Meddle. 'Shall I give you your medicine? You do look ill.'

'I feel it,' groaned his aunt. 'Yes, give me my medicine. It's in the blue bottle.'

Meddle got the bottle. 'How much do I pour you?' he asked.

'A tablespoonful,' said his aunt, lying with her eyes shut, looking very miserable indeed. Meddle poured out the medicine into a tablespoon. Then he held it out. 'Sit up, Aunt Jemima. Here's your medicine.'

She sat up, and Meddle held the spoon to her mouth. But as soon as she tasted it she gave a loud yell and knocked the spoon out of Meddle's hand. The medicine went all over him.

'Meddle! What's that? That isn't my nice, sweet cough medicine. It's HORRIBLE!'

'Well, you said the blue bottle,' said Meddle, holding it up. His aunt groaned, and lay down again.

'That's my eye-drops. You would get the wrong bottle! Couldn't you even look to see what the label says as plain as can be – *eye-drops.*'

'I'm sorry, Aunt,' said Meddle, picking up

another blue bottle. 'I'll give you the right medicine this time.'

'No, you won't. You won't give me anything at all, if I can help it,' said his aunt. 'All I want you to do is to go away as quickly as possible before you start meddling. Go home, Meddle, go home!'

'You sound as if I were a dog!' said Meddle indignantly. 'Please, Aunt, isn't there anything I can do? Don't you want any shopping done, for instance?'

'Yes, I do,' said his aunt, shutting her eyes again. 'But *you're* not going to do it, Meddle! I know what your shopping is like. Even if you take a list with you you always bring the wrong things back. Meddle and muddle, that's what you do! Go home!'

Meddle was very hurt. He went down the stairs and into the scullery. A voice followed him. 'And don't forget that the larder door squeaks, Meddle! I know when anyone is opening it!'

Meddle thought his aunt was being unfair. He wished he could show her she was wrong about him. Didn't he want to be helpful? Yes, he did! Then why wouldn't she let him at least do her shopping?

His eye caught sight of a list on the kitchen table. Ah! This must be Aunt Jemima's shopping list. Maybe she had just been going out shopping when she had fallen ill. Well, what about Mister Meddle taking the list, doing the shopping simply beautifully, and showing his Aunt Jemima that he really was a clever fellow after all?

He put his hand into his pocket. Had he got any money with him that morning? Yes, he had. His uncle had sent him quite a lot for his birthday the week before. Should he go shopping with his own money and get it back from his aunt afterwards – or should he go back upstairs and ask her for some shopping money?

'No. She wouldn't give me any – and she would still say I wasn't to do the shopping,' said Meddle to himself. 'I'll use my own – and when I come back with all the things on the list, she'll be so pleased with me that she'll give me a few extra pence for my trouble, as well as the money I have spent.'

He picked up the neat little list and went out of the house. He looked at the list as he went.

One small blue tablecloth. Well, that's easy.

I know just the kind she has! One tea-cloth. That's easy too, I can get it at the same shop. One white apron. Lucky I know the kind she wears in the morning! I'll have to get a nice big size for Aunt Jemima because she's rather fat. I'll go to the draper's for all these.'

He looked at the list again. 'One sheet. One pillowcase. One Turkish towel, small. Well, well – this is really quite a bit of luck. I can do all the shopping at the same shop! I'm sure the draper will sell all these.'

Meddle was pleased. This was very easy

shopping to do. He hoped he had enough money.

He went to the draper's and walked to the counter that sold towels and sheets and pillowcases.

'I want a nice white sheet, please, for a single bed, and a pillowcase to match, and a small Turkish towel,' said Meddle.

'Only *one* sheet, sir? asked the shop girl. 'We usually sell them in pairs.'

'Well, my aunt only wants *one*,' said Meddle, firmly. 'So one it must be.'

The shop girl managed to find an odd sheet, a plain pillowcase and a small Turkish towel.

'Anything else?' she asked.

'Oh, yes. One small blue tablecloth, one tea-cloth and a white apron, large size,' said Meddle, looking at his list. 'That's all. I'll take them with me.'

He had them wrapped up, and the girl gave him the bill. Oh dear – it took nearly all the money his uncle had sent him for his birthday. Never mind – Aunt Jemima would repay it all.

He went out of the shop, pleased with himself. Now Aunt Jemima would see how clever he could be at shopping! He was sure that he had got just the right things.

He went back to the house and let himself in at the back door.

Somebody else was there, too – the young man from the laundry. He was collecting the basket of washing.

'Good morning,' he said to Meddle. 'I've come for the laundry – but I can't find the washing list. Have you seen it?'

'No, I haven't,' said Meddle. The young man went to the bottom of the stairs and called loudly.

'Your nephew is here, Ma'am, and *he* can't find the washing list either. So I'll just take the washing without it, and make out a list for you myself.'

'Thank you,' called back Aunt Jemima, croakily. The young man went out and shut the door, carrying the basket on his shoulder. Meddle ran upstairs with his parcel, beaming all over his face.

'Aunt Jemima, I found your shopping list and I've been shopping for you! Look!'

'What *do* you mean?' said his aunt, amazed. Meddle undid the parcel in great haste, anxious to show all the things he had bought.

'One sheet. One tablecloth, blue. One apron. One tea-cloth. One Turkish towel. One pillowcase. There you are – and here's the bill. Now, don't say I make a muddle whenever I go shopping!'

Aunt Jemima stared at the things in astonishment. 'But why did you buy all these?' she said. 'I don't want them!'

'Well, they were on your shopping list downstairs!' said Meddle, and he pushed the list into his aunt's hands. 'See – they're all down there.'

'Meddle,' said his aunt, 'Meddle, are you *quite* mad? This is the *laundry* list – the list of things I was sending to be washed. No wonder the man couldn't find it. Is there any sense in taking a *washing* list and going out to *buy* all the things on it?'

'Oh, Aunt – I thought it was your shopping list!' wailed Meddle. 'I did really. Please pay me back for all I've bought.'

'Certainly not,' said his aunt. 'Take them home yourself and use them – and tie the apron round your waist when you do your washing-up! You'll look fine! Go home, Meddle. If you don't, I'll get up and take the broom to you!'

217

So now Meddle is going home with all the things he bought, because the shop won't take them back. He's very sad – he has wasted his money, and made such a muddle again. He never *will* learn not to meddle, will he?

Chapter 9

A Surprise for Mister Meddle

Mister Meddle was always meddling in things that were no business of his, and poking his nose in where he wasn't wanted.

But he got a great surprise when he went to stay with his cousins, Snip and Snap. They didn't like meddlers, they didn't like borrowers, and they got very impatient indeed with their cousin Meddle.

'Who's taken my new whipping-top?' said Snip. 'You, Meddle? Well, where is it then? Where have you put it?'

'Dear me – I'm sure I put it back on the shelf,' said Meddle. But it wasn't there, of course.

'Meddle! Did you borrow my watch?' asked Snap. 'I can't find it anywhere.'

'Dear me – yes, I did,' said Meddle, looking at his wrist. 'I wanted to be sure of catching my bus, you know. Oh, Snap – I'm sorry, but it must have slipped off my wrist.'

'Meddle, did you go and give the cat that milk pudding out of the larder?' called his Aunt Amanda. 'Or did you eat it yourself?'

'Oh, Aunt, the cat mewed so loudly and was so hungry I thought you'd *want* me to give it

something to eat,' said Meddle. 'And I don't much like milk pudding.'

'Well, other people do,' said his aunt crossly. 'Snip and Snap – you'll have to deal with Meddle for me. If he meddles much more I'll send him away!'

'If you take our things again and lose them or don't bring them back we'll use magic on *your* things – and we'll make them disappear!' said Snip to Meddle.

'Pooh!' said Meddle. 'You're only kids. You don't know any magic. You ought to be *pleased* when I bother myself with your things.'

'Well, we're not,' said Snap. 'Now remember, Meddle – the very next time you meddle with our things, we shall meddle with yours – and away they'll go under your very nose!'

Meddle didn't believe Snip and Snap. He took no notice of their threats at all. He just went on doing what he liked. He borrowed their ball to play with and it fell into a gutter on the roof of the house and couldn't be got down. He borrowed Snap's new socks and because they were too small he wore them into holes.

'He's hopeless,' said Snip to Snap. 'We'll

have to teach him a lesson. What about our wonderful Disappearing Trick?'

'Oooh, yes,' said Snap. 'We'll get our friends in to help. Let's call a meeting. We'll ask Tippy, Jinky, Impy and Heyho.'

So all those four met with Snip and Snap at Tippy's and talked about how to punish Meddle for his aggravating ways.

'We'll do the Disappearing Trick on him,' said Snip. 'We'll get his football, his cricket bat, his new pair of socks and his football boots. We'll tie long, long black thread to them, and tie the other ends to your bicycles.'

Snap began to giggle as he saw the surprised faces of the others.

'It's all right, we're not mad,' he said. 'It's a trick we've played before. Now you, Tippy, can have the socks tied to your bicycle. The black thread will be very long indeed, and won't be seen – so a long time after you've passed by on your bicycle the socks will come dragging along the road, looking as if they're coming all by themselves. You'll be out of sight, you see!'

Tippy laughed loudly. 'My, what a good trick! And I suppose you'll tie the other things to the other bicycles, and they'll come along the road, too!'

'Yes – we'll tie the boots to Jinky's bicycle, the football to Impy's and the cricket bat to Heyho's,' grinned Snip. 'You'll ride by one after another, you see, and Meddle won't *dream* that anything is tied to you. The socks will come wriggling along like snakes, the boots will come jiggling by, the football will bounce along all by itself and the cricket bat will race along like anything.'

Everyone began to laugh. Impy held his sides. 'My, this is the best joke I've ever heard of. When do we play it?'

'This evening,' said Snap. 'We'll get you the socks and all the other things this afternoon when Meddle is out, and we'll give you reels of black thread, too. You can each tie your things on, and then go to the little shed at the end of Jiminy Lane.'

'You'll see us walking by with Meddle,' said Snip. 'And that will be your signal to set out – one by one, mind, with about a minute's time between each. Leave us to do the rest!'

'I shall fall off my bicycle with laughing,' said Impy. 'I know I shall.'

'I'd love to see Meddle's face when his football comes bouncing by on its own!' said

Jinky.

Everyone went home, giggling. What a trick! Whatever would Meddle say?

Now, that evening, when everything was ready and prepared, Snip and Snap went to Meddle.

'Have you found my watch?' demanded Snap.

'What about my ball?' said Snip.

'Oh, go away,' said Meddle, crossly. 'You know I haven't found them. Leave me alone.

I'm going for my evening walk and I don't want you.'

But Snip and Snap went with him. They went down the lane, and passed the little shed. Inside were Tippy, Jinky, Impy and Heyho waiting impatiently with their bicycles. Tied to the backs of them with long black thread were all the things belonging to Meddle!

'Meddle, we're going to teach you a lesson,' said Snip, solemnly. 'We're going to work some magic here tonight, and send away some of the things you like best – things belonging to *you*!'

'Oh, don't be silly,' said Meddle. 'Go home! As if *you* knew any magic!'

'Meddle,' said Snap, in such a peculiar voice that Meddle stopped, startled. 'Meddle! Would you like to see your new socks, your football boots, your football and your cricket bat all disappear?'

'Don't talk nonsense,' said Meddle uneasily. 'And let me tell you that if you take them from my room and hide them, I'll tell your mother!'

'Oh, we won't hide them!' said Snip. 'We'll call them from your room this very minute –

and we'll send them rushing up the road as fast as can be – off to the Land of Rubbish, as sure as eggs are eggs!'

'I don't believe a word of it,' said Meddle, scornfully. 'If I *see* my socks rushing by, I'll believe it, certainly – but not until. Magic like that isn't learnt by kids like you!'

A bicycle came down the lane. Tippy was riding it. Snip and Snap didn't smile at him, and he didn't wave to them. Meddle didn't know him.

'Just wait till this bicycle's gone by,' said Snip. 'Ah, he's gone. Now then – SOCKS, COME BY AND RUN AWAY!'

Something black and wriggly now appeared a little way down the road. It was Meddle's socks, tied to the distant bicycle with long black thread. The thread couldn't be seen – but here came the socks, wriggling along fast like excited black snakes!

They passed in half a moment, and Meddle clutched at Snip and Snap in horror.

'Oooh! I say they *did* look like my socks! Snip, is it magic? Snap, don't do this. I don't like it. Were those really my socks?'

'Of course,' said Snip, trying not to laugh. He saw the next bicycle coming, with Jinky in the saddle. He nudged Snap.

'And now I think we'll call for Meddle's football boots to come!' said Snap. 'BOOTS, COME BY AND RUN AWAY!'

Jinky had gone by on his bicycle, grinning, but not looking at Snip or Snap. Meddle looked down the road in alarm. What was this jigging along? Could it be – could it *really* be – his football boots?

'It is, it is! It's my boots!' cried poor Meddle, looking quite pale. 'Oh, stop, boots! Stop! There they go, my lovely boots!'

And there they went, jigging along the road on the black thread, Jinky's distant bicycle pulling them fast. They looked most peculiar.

'Snip! Snap! Don't do any more magic,' wailed Meddle. 'I don't like it. It's horrible. I've lost my socks and now my boots.'

Impy came by on his bicycle next, pedalling fast, afraid that he might explode into laughter at the sight of Meddle's face. Snip called out, as soon as he had gone by:

'FOOTBALL, COME BY AND RUN AWAY!'

'No, no!' begged Meddle. 'Not my football. Not my fine, splendid football! Oh, my, oh, my – it's coming! It's coming, as sure as anything! And I daren't stop it, I daren't. I'm afraid I might go off to the Land of Rubbish, too!'

Snip and Snap turned away to laugh. The football bounced along like a live thing, leaping high in the air if it touched a stone or a rut. It went by at top speed, and Meddle sat down on the kerb and groaned.

'Snip and Snap, I'll never meddle with your things again, never. Please, please, stop this. I'm frightened. I'm very – oh, my goodness me, is this something else coming?'

Heyho had cycled by, and behind him at a good distance came the cricket bat, sliding along fairly smoothly, but giving little jigs when it passed over a stone. Snip giggled. Meddle covered his face with his hands as soon as he heard Snap shouting to the bat to come by and run away.

'There goes my wonderful bat! Is there no end to this? Snip, forgive me. Now that I see my own treasures rushing off to the Land of Rubbish I know how you must have felt when I lost your ball and your watch and spoilt your socks, and gave your pudding to the cat, and –'

'All right. We'll stop the magic now,' said

Snip, with another giggle. 'We did think of sending your trunk off, too, but we thought we'd better not, or you might live with us the rest of your life if you'd no trunk to pack to go away.'

'I'm going away,' said Meddle. 'I'm leaving you tomorrow. You're too magic for me! I'd be afraid of ever borrowing anything again. And do you know what I'm going to do before I go?'

'No. What?' asked Snip and Snap.

'I'm going to get some money out of my bank,' said Meddle, 'and I'm going to buy a

new watch and a new ball, and new socks for
you, and all the things I've ever borrowed and
lost I'll buy and give you. This has been a
lesson to me. My goodness – how magic you
are!'

Snip and Snap were surprised to hear all
this. They looked at one another, feeling
rather awkward.

'Well, if you really are sorry – and will really
buy us all the things you've borrowed and
spoilt and lost – maybe we'll use our magic to

get back the things of yours that have rushed by this evening, and disappeared,' said Snip.

Meddle beamed. 'Will you really? That's grand of you! I'm afraid of going to the Land of Rubbish to fetch them.'

'Yes. They might keep you there,' said Snap, and giggled. 'All right, Meddle, it's a bargain – you buy us new things in place of the ones you've lost or spoilt and we'll get all *your* things back for you!'

Well, of course, it was easy to get them back, as you can imagine! They just went round to Tippy's the next day, and found Tippy, Jinky, Impy and Heyho there with all the things quite safe – and what a laugh they had together when they remembered how everything had rushed by the night before!

Meddle went out that morning, got some money and bought a whole lot of new things. He gave them to Snip and Snap and his Aunt Amanda. He packed his trunk. He sent a note to the station to ask a porter to fetch it. He really seemed quite a different person!

He was very glad to have his socks, boots, ball and bat back. He looked at Snip and Snap in awe and admiration.

'I never knew you were so magic,' he said.

'You frighten me! My word, I'm going to be careful in future!'

He said goodbye and off he went, swinging his stick in the air.

'I say,' said Snip, suddenly. 'Meddle lost his stick last week. Whose stick was that? It wasn't our *very best one*, was it?'

They rushed to the hall-stand to see if their stick was there. It was gone. Their mother called out to them.

'Meddle has borrowed it. He says he'll send it back next week.'

But will he? Snip and Snap can't make up their minds if he will or not – and neither can I! *What* a joke they played on Meddle, didn't they? I wish I'd been there to see it.

Chapter 10

Goodbye, Mister Meddle

Mister Meddle always liked roaming round the railway station. It was a most exciting place, with trains puffing in and out, people hurrying all about, and porters shouting, 'Mind your backs, please!'

One morning he went into the station, and sat down on a seat to watch what was going on. He saw the people buying their tickets, carrying their luggage, looking for their trains.

'They all look very worried,' said Meddle to himself. 'Very worried indeed. Perhaps I'd better help some of them.'

Now, Meddle, as you know, was exactly like his name. If he could poke his long nose into anything and meddle with it, he was happy! So up he got to see what he could do.

He met a little man panting and puffing, carrying a very heavy bag. Meddle went up to him and tried to get hold of it. 'Let me help,' he said.

'Certainly not. Let go,' said the man, fiercely. 'I know what you'd do if I let you take my bag – run off with it! And that's the last I would see of it.'

'What a dreadful thing to say!' said Meddle, and stalked off crossly. He bumped into a woman who was carrying three parcels and dragging a little dog along too. 'Allow me, Madam!' said Meddle politely, and took the biggest parcel from the woman.

The dog immediately flew at him and nipped his leg. Meddle dropped the parcel and howled. There was crash!

'There now!' said the woman, angrily. 'I had my best glass bowls packed in that parcel! What do you think you are doing, snatching it from me?'

'Your horrible dog bit me,' said Meddle, most annoyed.

'Well, of course he did!' said the woman. 'He thought you were stealing my parcel. It served you right. Please call a porter and ask him to clear up this mess of broken glass –

and you will have to pay me five pounds for breaking the bowls.'

A porter came up. 'I saw you meddling!' he said to Meddle. 'If parcels want carrying, *I'll* carry them. It's my job, not yours. And *you* can clear up the mess, because that's your job, not mine!'

Well, you would have thought that Meddle would have had enough of poking his nose into other people's affairs by then, wouldn't you? Not a bit of it! He paid the angry woman five pounds, he cleared up the mess – and then he went around looking for somebody else to meddle with.

He saw a little man, a big, plump woman, and four children all trailing along. 'Oh dear, oh dear!' said the woman. 'We shall miss the train, I know! Where do we get our tickets?'

'Madam, over there,' said Meddle, hurrying up to her. 'Shall I hold the children's hands while you get them?'

'No, thank you,' said the woman. 'They can hold each other's hands. Dad, get your money ready for the tickets. Oh dear, what a queue there is at the ticket office!'

'Madam, you go and get your seats in the train and I'll buy the tickets for you,' said Meddle.

'Do go away!' said the little man, crossly. 'I'm not leaving you here with my money, I wouldn't be so silly!'

'That's not a nice thing to say at all!' said Meddle, most offended. 'Do you mean to say I'd run off with the money? Well, I never heard such a –'

'Do please go away,' said the plump woman. 'We can look after ourselves all right. Oh my, oh my, what a queue. I wish these people in front of us would hurry up, I know we shall miss our train.'

'We'll catch it all right,' said the little man,

looking at the station clock. 'But if its crowded we shan't get any seats, that's certain.'

The children began to cry. 'I want a seat,' sobbed one. 'I want to look out of the window.'

'Shall I go and get some seats for you?' said Meddle, quite determined to help in some way. 'I could go and find a carriage and put newspapers and things on six seats – then no one would take those seats, and when you came along you could have them. I could hop out of the carriage and wave goodbye.'

'What an extraordinary fellow!' said the little man to his wife. He turned to Meddle. 'I tell you, we don't want people poking their noses into our business,' he said. 'We can't stop you finding seats, of course, and spreading them with newspapers and coats to keep them for us! I can see you mean to interfere with us in *some* way!'

'Not interfere – just *help*,' said Meddle, quite hurt. 'All right – I'm off to get some seats for you. I'll buy some newspapers to spread on them, so that people will know they are all reserved for others!'

He turned away, pleased. He bought some

papers and then ran to find the train. Bother! He had forgotten to ask which one it was. It must be the very next train leaving, because the little man and his wife were in such a hurry to get the tickets. One of the children had said they were going to the sea – now which train would it be?

'Ah – here's one leaving in five minutes – to Seaside Town,' said Meddle. 'This must be it. How glad they will be when they come rushing on to the platform, find the train is full – but with six seats saved for them!'

He bought a platform ticket and hurried to the train. He found a carriage that was quite empty. Good! He sat down, and arranged four newspapers and his overcoat on five seats. He sat in the sixth himself, of course.

He felt pleased with himself. 'It's so nice to help people,' he said. 'Now that little family will all travel comfortably to the seaside, each with a nice seat all the way.'

People looked into the carriage, saw the newspapers and coat on the seats and went on again. Meddle grinned. Aha! He had been very clever, he thought.

The minutes went by. Meddle began to feel anxious. Surely those people wouldn't miss the train? He looked out of the door. There was no sign of them. Oh dear – should he go and hurry them up?

Meddle got out some pennies to give to the children when they came. One fell from his hand and rolled under the seat. Oh dear! Meddle got down to get it. It was right in the far corner. Meddle had to get half-way under the seat to reach it.

A loud whistle blew. PHEEEEEEEE! Meddle jumped. He tried to wriggle out from under the seat, but somehow or other he got stuck. 'Wait, wait! Tell the train not to go yet!' shouted Meddle, from under the seat. But nobody heard him, of course. The guard blew his whistle again and then, with a rattle and a rumble and clatter, the train began to pull out of the station!

Meddle wriggled himself free and rushed to the window. He leaned out, shouting loudly, trying to open the door. It was a good thing he couldn't because the train was now going quite fast.

'Stop! Stop! Let me out!' yelled Meddle. 'I'm not going, I tell you!'

But he was. He couldn't help it! And the last thing that poor Meddle saw was the little man and his family all getting calmly into another train marked 'To Golden Sands' – and finding plenty of seats, too!

'This *wasn't* their train!' groaned poor Meddle. 'And *what* will the ticket inspector say to me if he comes and finds me without a proper ticket and all the seats to myself? Oh dear – this is what comes of helping people.'

No, Meddle – that's what comes of meddling! There he goes, all the way to the sea, first stop Seaside Town!

Mister Meddle's Muddles

Mister Meddle's

Muddles

Enid Blyton

Illustrations by Diana Catchpole

BLOOMSBURY
CHILDREN'S
BOOKS

Contents

Chapter 1

Mister Meddle Makes a Muddle

Once, when Meddle was staying with his Aunt Jemima, he broke one of her chairs. She was very cross about it.

'Meddle, you are very careless,' she said. 'I can't imagine how you broke that chair. It was quite strong.'

'It fell over and broke itself,' said Meddle.

'Somebody must have pushed it,' said Aunt Jemima. 'Well, it's not worth mending. It's got two legs and the back broken. I must go out this morning and buy another chair. And whilst I'm about it, I may as well get another little table for the kitchen corner there. It would be useful to put trays on. And I really need a new stool for my feet. I'll go and get them straight away.'

247

'Shall I come with you and carry them back for you, Aunt Jemima?' asked Meddle, anxious to make up for his carelessness.

'No, thank you,' said his aunt. 'You don't suppose I want them dropped all over the road and broken before they get home, do you? I shall tell the shop to send them when their van goes out this morning. You stay here and open the door when the van comes.'

So Meddle stayed at home whilst his aunt went out. He stood at the window watching for the van to come. At last he heard a rumbling down the street and along came a heavy van. It stopped at the house next door, which was empty. Meddle tapped on the window.

'Hi!' he called. 'This is the house. Hi, deliver the goods here, please. I am waiting for them.

The man got down from the van and looked doubtfully at Meddle. 'Are you sure, sir?' he asked. 'We were told to deliver at Number 8 – and your house is 6.'

'Of course I'm sure!' said Meddle, crossly. 'I've stood here all the morning waiting for you. I'll give you a hand with the things if you like.'

'Well, my mate is here,' said the man, and he whistled to a man at the back of the van. 'This is the house,' he called. 'I'll back the van a bit and then we'll get the goods out.'

So the big van was backed a little and then the two men got to work. First they carried in a fine armchair.

'My word!' thought Meddle. 'Aunt Jemima has got a much nicer chair than the one I broke. It's a beauty. I shall like to sit and snooze in that in the evening.'

The men went back to the van and brought out a table. It was very big. Meddle stared at it in surprise. 'Well, I quite thought Aunt

Jemima would have bought a small one,' he said to himself. 'This will almost fill up the whole kitchen!'

'It's to go in the kitchen,' he told the men, and he led the way. It really did almost fill up the little room!

The men went back to the van and came out with a bed, taken to pieces. Meddle stared at it. 'Well, what's Aunt bought a bed for?' he wondered. 'She didn't say anything about a bed. I wonder where it's to go. Well, there are only two bedrooms, and hers is the bigger, so it had better go in there!'

That wasn't the end of Meddle's surprise. The men brought a sofa out of the van, some more chairs, a sideboard, some stools, some carpets, another table and heaps of pictures!

'Aunt Jemima must have gone mad!' thought Meddle, telling the men to put the things here and there. 'Yes, she must have gone quite mad! She set out to buy a chair, a little table, and a stool – and she seems to have bought a whole houseful of furniture! It's really very puzzling.'

'Well, that's the lot, sir,' said the men, and Meddle gave them five pounds. The van drove off and Meddle was left alone with all the furniture. He could really hardly move in the house, it was so crammed with chairs and tables and things!

Aunt Jemima came home at half-past twelve carrying a bag full of shopping. She let herself into the house and then stared in the greatest surprise at the hall. Usually there was a hall stand there and nothing else. But now there were two chairs, a roll of carpet, and a small table!

'Meddle!' she called. 'Meddle, what are these things doing here?'

'Well, I didn't know where you wanted them to be put, Aunt,' said Meddle. 'Just tell me, and I'll take them wherever you like!'

'Meddle, I don't want them put anywhere!' cried his aunt. 'I don't know anything about them.'

'But you bought them, didn't you?' said Meddle, in surprise. 'Aunt Jemima, do you feel all right? I must say I was rather astonished to find you had bought so much furniture this morning!'

'Are you mad, Meddle?' said his aunt, beginning to look at him in a way he didn't like at all. 'I bought what I said I'd buy this morning – a chair, a little table, and a stool.

Nothing else at all. And they can't be delivered till tomorrow. Now perhaps you will kindly tell me where all these things came from?'

'Aunt Jemima – Aunt Jemima – this is all very strange,' said Meddle, staring around at the furniture. His aunt went into the sitting-room and looked in amazement at everything there. She could hardly move.

'Meddle, what in the world have you been doing?' she said at last. 'I know you do the silliest things, but I can't think how you have managed to get all this furniture here like this, this morning. Where did it come from?'

'Two men brought it,' said Meddle. He was beginning to feel most uncomfortable.

Just then a knock came at the door. Aunt Jemima opened it. A little woman stood outside, looking rather worried.

'I'm so sorry to trouble you,' she said. 'But we are moving in next door and our furniture van hasn't come along yet. I suppose you haven't seen it, have you?'

Then Aunt Jemima guessed everything. Silly old Meddle had taken in the furniture that should have gone next door! How exactly like him! If he could meddle, he would – and his meddles always made such muddles!

'I believe a dreadful mistake has been made,' said Aunt Jemima. 'I was out this morning and my stupid nephew has taken in your furniture here.'

'Why – yes – it's my furniture!' cried the little woman, staring round the hall in surprise. 'Oh dear – and I've been waiting for it. The men are gone. Whatever shall I do?'

'Meddle shall carry it next door himself and put it wherever you want it,' said Aunt Jemima firmly. 'Meddle, do you hear me? It's no good your slinking off into the garden like that. Come back. You've made a fine old muddle and you're just going to put it right!'

'But I can't carry heavy furniture about!' cried poor Meddle, looking round at the chairs and tables in a fright.

'Well, you're going to,' said his aunt. 'Now begin right away, please, because I want to hang up my coat and hat and I can't possibly get into my bedroom until some of the things are taken from the landing!'

So poor Meddle spent the rest of the day grunting and groaning under the heavy furniture, carrying it piece by piece into the house next door. How tired he was when the evening came! He sank down into a chair and sighed heavily.

'I'm not a bit sorry for you, Meddle,' said his aunt. 'Not a bit. You just won't learn sense. You didn't use your brains this morning, so you've had to use your arms and your legs and your back, and tire them out! Perhaps next time you will use your brains and save yourself a lot of trouble.'

'I will,' said Meddle. 'I certainly will!'

But, if I know Meddle, he certainly won't!

Chapter 2

Mister Meddle Is a Snowman

One day Mister Meddle met his friend Jinks. Jinks was looking very cross, and Meddle was surprised.

'What's the matter, Jinks?' he asked.

'Someone's been taking the onions out of my garden shed,' said Jinks. 'I saw their footsteps in the snow this morning. I feel very cross.'

'You should catch the thief, Jinks,' said Meddle.

'All very well to say that, but he's gone,' said Jinks.

'Well, he may come again. Can't you hide under a bush in the garden and watch for him?' asked Meddle.

'What, sit out there in the cold every frosty

night, and have snow fall down my neck and the frost biting my fingers and toes? Don't be silly, Meddle,' said Jinks, and he went off with his nose in the air.

Meddle stared after him. He didn't like to be called silly. 'Oh, all right, Jinks, if you're so high and mighty I won't try to help you,' said Meddle, and he marched off too.

But on the way home a perfectly marvellous idea hopped into his head. He stopped and thought about it.

'I believe it's just the idea for catching the thief!' said Meddle. 'If I pretend to be a snowman and stand still in the middle of Jinks's front garden, I shall be able to watch and see if the robber comes in. And he won't mind me at all, because he'll think I'm only a snowman. What a wonderful idea!'

He thought about it. How could he make himself like a snowman? He didn't think it would be very pleasant to cover himself with snow on such a cold night. No – he wouldn't have snow.

'I could wear my big, new, white mackintosh cape!' thought Meddle suddenly. 'Of course! It would make me look like a snowman! What a splendid idea! And I could rub flour all over my face and make it white. And wear my own hat – snowmen always wear hats. They have sticks, too, so I can take my stick to hit the robber with.'

Meddle felt very excited. He rushed home and got out his mackintosh. It covered him almost to the ground, so it would do very well.

'How pleased Jinks will be when I catch the robber for him!' thought Meddle. 'He'll be sorry he marched off with his nose in the air!'

That night Meddle crept down the road, with his mackintosh cape rolled up under his arm and his face white with flour. He didn't

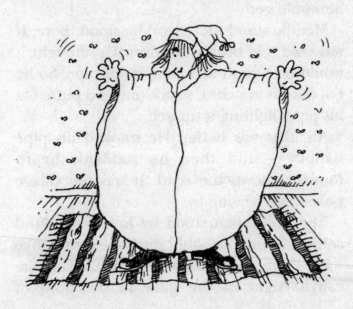

mean to put the mackintosh on until he came to Jinks's garden.

When he got there, there was no one about. So Meddle unrolled his big, white cape and put it round his shoulders.

It fell almost to his feet. He kept his hat on, and he had a scarf round his neck to keep out the cold. Snowmen often had scarves.

Well, there he stood in Jinks's front garden, dressed in white, with his hat and scarf on – and a pipe in his mouth, too, though it wasn't lit. He stood there feeling most important. Now let the robber come – and what a shock he would get!

Meddle stood there, and he stood there. It was cold. He began to shiver. He thought it would be a good idea to light his pipe. So he got out his matches, struck one and puffed at his pipe, lighting it up well.

Ah, that was better. He smoked his pipe happily – and then he suddenly heard footsteps down the road. It was the village policeman passing by.

The policeman stood by Jinks's gate and sniffed. Funny, he could smell tobacco smoke – but there was nobody about at all. Then he caught sight of the glow in the bowl of

Meddle's pipe. Goodness! Somebody was standing in Jinks's garden smoking – but there was no one there except the snowman.

'How can a snowman smoke a pipe?' wondered the policeman, puzzled. 'How strange!'

He thought he would go into the garden and see what could be happening. So he opened the gate quietly and crept into the garden.

Now Meddle had no idea it was the village policeman. When he heard footsteps and then heard the gate open and someone coming inside, he at once thought it must be the robber!

'Ah!' he thought. 'Now I'll give him a shock!'

So he walked forward two or three steps and yelled, 'Stop, there!'

The policeman got a dreadful shock. He had never in his life before seen a snowman that walked and talked. He stood still in fright, and couldn't say a word.

The snowman walked right up to him. The policeman simply couldn't bear it. He gave a yell and tore out of the gate and down the street. Meddle quite thought he must be the

robber, and he tore after him, stumbling over his long, white cape.

'Help! The snowman's after me! The snowman's after me!' yelled the frightened policeman. People came running out of their houses to see what was happening, and when they saw the snowman rushing after the policeman, they were so frightened that they ran away too.

And soon Meddle found himself chasing quite a crowd of people. He began to enjoy himself. It was fun to make so many people run!

'Stop, stop!' he yelled. But nobody stopped. They ran on and on. The policeman got to the police station. He stumbled in, panting out that a snowman was chasing him – and all the other policemen put on their helmets and ran out to see. They were just in time to see the frightened people rushing past – and there was the snowman galloping after them!

One policeman put out his foot as Meddle thundered past. Meddle tripped and fell over, rolling along the pavement. He was very angry.

'How dare you trip me up!' he yelled. 'I was after the robber! Now he's escaped.'

The policeman dragged Meddle into the police station. The frightened policeman, who had ran away, was most astonished to see him.

'So you weren't a snowman after all!' he said. 'You were dressed up in that white cape. Well, Mister Meddle, and what were you doing in Mister Jinks's garden, I should like to know? I suppose you weren't looking for his onions, by any chance?'

'How dare you say that,' cried Meddle. 'I was watching for the thief – and I thought you were the thief – and that's why I chased you!'

'Well, Mister Meddle, please don't go about

pretending to be a snowman any more,' said the head policeman. 'You've caused enough trouble for one night, meddling like this. Anyway, Mister Jinks has locked up his shed and taken the key, so nobody can steal his onions again. You needn't bother yourself with the robber either – we caught him this evening, stealing somebody's leeks.'

'Well, really! So all my trouble was for nothing!' said Meddle indignantly. 'And I've torn my white cape and somebody's trodden on my hat – all for nothing. It's too bad.'

'It's your own fault,' said the policeman. 'You shouldn't meddle!'

'Ho!' said Meddle haughtily, and off he went home, sticking his nose high in the air. He'll never learn, will he?

Chapter 3

Mister Meddle and the Bull

Did you ever hear about Mister Meddle and the bull? It's really rather funny.

Well, one day Mister Meddle got up feeling good. 'I'd like to do a good deed today,' he thought. 'I'd like to help an old woman across the road, or carry a heavy parcel for someone, or jump into the river and save somebody from drowning. I feel good enough for all those things.'

He went out to do his shopping as usual, and he looked about for a runaway horse that he could stop. But all his horses trotted along properly and not one ran away. So that was no good.

Then he walked by the river to see if

anyone would fall in so that he could rescue them. But nobody did.

Then he looked about for anyone carrying a heavy parcel, but the only person he saw was Mr Grumps, so he pretended not to notice he was carrying anything at all.

He waited about to see if any old ladies wanted to be helped over the road, but all the old ladies he saw seemed quite able to run across by themselves. So that wasn't any good either.

Mister Meddle was most disappointed. He went home by the fields, and in the distance he saw Farmer Barley, and he thought he would ask him if he could help him at all. The farmer was in the next field but one, so Mister Meddle opened the gate of the nearest field and shut it behind him, meaning to walk across to see the farmer.

The farmer heard the click of the gate and turned to look over the hedge to see who it was.

'I say!' began Meddle shouting loudly. 'Do you want –'

But Farmer Barley didn't wait to hear what Meddle said. He yelled over the hedge: 'Mind that bull!'

Meddle looked all round, but he couldn't see any bull. The farmer shouted again.

'Didn't you hear me telling you to mind that bull?'

'Now why does he want me to mind his bull!' wondered Meddle. 'Oh – I suppose he wants to go home to his dinner or something, and would like me to mind the bull for him whilst he goes. Well, as I'm looking for something good to do, I'll do what he says.'

Meddle yelled back to Farmer Barley, 'All right. I'll mind the bull! Don't worry!'

'Right!' said the farmer, and went off down

the field towards his farm. Meddle still couldn't see any bull, though he looked hard.

But the bull had seen him! It was in a little cluster of trees, and it didn't like the look of Meddle at all!

Meddle suddenly saw the bull looking at him. He decided that it didn't look a very kind animal.

'In fact, it looks rather fierce,' thought Meddle. 'Well, I'll mind it for the farmer, but I hope it won't try to run away, or anything, because I should just hate to try and bring it back.'

The bull glared at Meddle and snorted down its nose.

'You needn't do that at me,' said Meddle to the bull. 'That's a rude noise to make at anyone minding you. Don't worry. I shan't come any nearer to you. I shall stay here and you can stay there.'

But the bull didn't think the same as Meddle! It came out of the trees with a run and snorted at Meddle again, whisking its big tail up into the air.

'I wonder if bulls are pleased when they wag their tails,' thought Meddle, feeling rather uncomfortable. 'Dogs are, I know –

but this bull doesn't look at all pleased as he wags his tail. Not a bit pleased. In fact, he looks awfully angry.'

Meddle moved away a bit. The bull moved a little nearer and gave such an alarming snort that Meddle almost jumped out of his skin.

'You're making it very difficult for me to mind you!' he shouted to the bull. 'Do behave yourself. I'm only minding you till the farmer comes back.'

The bull made up his mind that he couldn't bear Meddle in his field one minute

longer. So he snorted again and ran headlong at him, putting his head down in a horrid manner. Meddle took one look at the bull's horns and fled!

How he ran! He tore to the gate with the bull after him, and got there just as the bull did. The bull tried to help him over the gate with his horns and tore Meddle's trousers, making a big hole. Meddle tumbled to the other side of the gate with a bump. The bull put his head over the top bar and snorted all over Meddle.

'You are a disgusting and most ungrateful animal,' said Meddle angrily. 'Look what you've done to my trousers! And all because I was doing a good deed and minding you for the farmer. Well – I'm not minding you any more, so you can just do what you like! I'm going to complain about you to the farmer!'

So Meddle marched off to the farmhouse, feeling very angry indeed. He rapped on the door and the farmer opened it.

'What's the matter?' he asked.

'Plenty!' said Meddle. 'Look at my trousers – new last week, and that bull of yours chased me and tore them!'

'Well, I told you to mind him,' said the

farmer. 'You should have got out of the field before he came for you.'

'Well, I thought it would be better to mind him for you in the field,' said Meddle. 'That's what comes of trying to do you a good turn.'

'What's all this about a good turn?' said the farmer, astonished. 'I didn't want you to do me a good turn! I wanted you to get out of that field as quickly as possible before the bull turned on you. When I told you to *mind* the bull I meant you to look out that he didn't chase you!'

'Well, why didn't you say so?' said Meddle, in a rage. He turned to go and nearly fell over a fat pig.

'Mind that pig now – mind that pig!' cried the farmer.

Poor Meddle! He does get into trouble, doesn't he!

Chapter 4

Mister Meddle Has a Surprise

Mister Meddle once went to stay with his Aunt Jemima, who was very strict with him. She thought it did him good, and no doubt it did – but Meddle didn't like it at all.

His Aunt Jemima did a lot of good works. She went to read to sick people, and she took pies and soups to the poor. She knitted socks for the soldiers, and did everything she could to help other people.

When Meddle came to stay with her, she made him help her. 'You can surely do a bit of knitting,' she said. 'It's easy enough.'

But poor Meddle somehow managed to get the wool all tangled round him and lost his needles. 'Are you trying to knit yourself as well as the wool?' asked his aunt crossly, as she untangled him.

'Perhaps it would be better if I took your pies and soups out?' said Meddle, thinking that it would be much easier to carry a basket than to knit a sock.

'Well, you can't make quite such a muddle with a pie as you can with wool, I suppose,' said Aunt Jemima. 'I am making a meat pie tomorrow for poor old Mrs Cook, who is in bed with a bad leg and can't do anything for herself. You shall come with me to see her, and carry the basket for me.'

'All right, Aunt Jemima,' said Meddle, with a sigh. 'I'll come.'

So the next day Aunt Jemima made a lovely round pie, with crust on it and a pretty pattern round the edge. She took it out of the oven, and showed it to Meddle.

'I wish we could have it for dinner,' said Meddle longingly.

'Don't be greedy!' said his aunt. 'Now just put it into that basket with a lid, Meddle. It's in the cupboard over there.'

Meddle found the basket. It was oblong, and had a lid that shut down, so that whatever was inside was safe from cats or dogs. 'Put the pie in, Meddle!' called his aunt. 'And don't forget to shut the lid down. I'm going up to put on my hat. You can wait for me in the garden.'

Meddle put the pie into the basket – but he forgot to shut down the lid. He went into the garden and put the basket down for a moment whilst he unpegged his scarf from the line. He felt to see if it was dry. It was, so he knotted it round his neck.

Now, whilst he was fiddling about with his scarf, a big blackbird flew down to the basket. It put its head on one side and looked at the pie. It looked good! The blackbird stood on the pie and pecked at the crust. Beaks and tails, it was delicious!

Meddle heard his aunt coming. He remembered that she told him to be sure to shut down the lid of the basket, and he hurriedly kicked it shut with his foot. He didn't see the blackbird inside! The surprised bird found itself shut in. It went on pecking at the pie, planning to fly out as soon as the lid was opened.

'Meddle! Aren't you ready?' cried Aunt Jemima. 'Come along now. You always seem to keep me waiting.'

Meddle picked up the basket and ran down the path to join his aunt. 'Come along, come along!' she said. 'We shall miss the bus.'

'Oh, are we going to catch the bus?' said Meddle, pleased. He always liked a ride in the bus or the train. 'Oh, good!'

He trotted along beside his aunt, swinging his basket, looking out for the bus. The blackbird inside didn't at all like being swung about like that. It gave aloud cheep. Meddle was most surprised.

He looked down at the basket. But the blackbird said no more for a while, Meddle and his aunt came to the bus stop. The bus was not in sight so they both sat down on the seat.

Meddle put the basket on his knee, for he was afraid he might forget it if he put it down on the seat. The blackbird began pecking again at the crust. Peck, peck, peck!

Meddle had sharp ears. He listened to the peck-peck-peck in surprise. 'Your pie does make a funny noise,' he said to his aunt. She stared at him in surprise.

'Meddle, I do hope you're not in one of your silly moods this morning,' she said to him sharply. 'You know quite well that pies don't make a noise.'

'Cheep-cheep!' said the blackbird. Meddle looked at the basket in astonishment. His aunt was a bit deaf, so she hadn't heard anything.

'Your pie is saying "Cheep-cheep",' he told his aunt.

'That's nothing to what *you'll* be saying in a minute when I scold you hard,' said his aunt crossly. 'Telling me that pies say cheep-cheep! Hold your tongue, Meddle!'

The blackbird thought it would sing a little song. So it swelled out its black throat,

opened its yellow beak and trilled out a dear
little tune:

'Tirra, tirra, ju-dy, ju-dee, dooit!'

'Aunt Jemima, I do wish you'd carry this pie
yourself,' said Meddle, beginning to feel
alarmed. 'It's beginning to sing now!'

'*Meddle*! If you don't stop telling me
ridiculous things, I'll box your big ears!' said
his aunt, in a real temper. 'Pies that sing –
what next?'

Luckily for Meddle, the bus came along at
that moment and they got in. Meddle badly
wanted to put the basket down on a seat, for
he was beginning to be afraid of it now, but
the bus was full, so he had to take the basket
on his knee once more.

The blackbird was rather frightened by the
noise of the bus, so it didn't cheep or sing for
a while. But when the bus stopped, it gave a
loud whistle. It was so loud that Aunt Jemima
heard it. She turned to Meddle at once.

'Stop whistling! A bus is not the place to
whistle in.'

'I didn't whistle,' said poor Meddle.

'Well, who did then?' said his aunt.

'The pie did,' said Meddle! His aunt glared at him. 'Meddle! Will you stop trying to be funny? First you tell me the pie cheeps – then you say it sings – and now you say it whistles! You'll be telling me it can fly next!'

Well, the blackbird took it into its head to flutter its wings and try to fly out of the basket at that moment. Meddle heard the fluttering wings in horror. Why, the pie was really doing what his aunt had said – it was flying round

and round the basket. Meddle began to tremble like a jelly, and his aunt felt him shivering against her.

'Meddle, do keep still! You are making me feel all funny, shaking like that! Whatever is the matter with you this morning?'

'It's the pie,' said poor Meddle. 'It's flying round the basket now.'

Aunt Jemima thought Meddle must be going mad. She was very glad when the bus stopped and they got out. Mrs Cook's house was quite near by. Meddle carried the basket there and thankfully put it on the table. Old Mrs Cook was in bed and she stared greedily at the basket. She felt sure that something good was in there!

'Good morning, Mrs Cook! I hope you are better!' said Aunt Jemima. 'I've brought you a pie. I can't think what's the matter with Meddle this morning, because he keeps saying that my pie cheeps, and sings, and whistles – and flies!'

The blackbird whistled loudly again. Aunt Jemima thought it was Meddle, and she scolded him. 'Now don't you dare to tell me that was the pie again!' she said. 'Open the basket and put the pie on a plate.'

But Meddle simply didn't dare to open the basket and touch that pie. He stood there, staring at his aunt, and she thought that really he must be going to be ill. So she opened the lid herself, in a rage.

And out flew the big blackbird and circled round her head! Aunt Jemima gave a scream. Mrs Cook squealed for all she was worth – and Meddle tried to run for the door and fell headlong over a stool.

He got up and looked sternly at his aunt. 'You bad woman! You cooked a blackbird in your pie! You bad woman! I suppose you remembered the twenty-four blackbirds that were baked in a pie – and you caught one and put it in! No wonder that pie sang and whistled and flew! Aunt Jemima, I'm *surprised* at you!'

And for once his aunt hadn't a single word to say. She just couldn't make it out at all.

Meddle looked into the basket and then took out the pie. The bird had pecked an enormous hole in the crust. 'Look there!' said Meddle, pointing to the hole. 'That's the hole the bird pecked so that it could get out of the pie. I think you are a most unkind person, Aunt Jemima!'

He stalked out of the house and went home – and whenever his aunt scolded him after that, Meddle would stare hard at her and say, 'Blackbirds! I haven't forgotten that, Aunt Jemima!'

And his Aunt Jemima wouldn't say a word more!

Chapter 5

Mister Meddle and the Chestnuts

Mister Meddle was very fond of roast chestnuts. He liked to make a little hole in them and put them down as close to the fire as he could without getting them burnt.

Then, when they were quite cooked through with the heat of the fire, he poked them away from the burning coal and let them cool in the fender. Then he peeled them, popped the delicious roasted nuts into his mouth and ate them.

But this year there were no chestnuts in the shops. Mister Meddle was very sad. He told his friend Jinky about it.

'You know, I'm going to miss my roast chestnuts very much,' he said. 'I just can't seem to buy any anywhere.'

'Well, don't you know any trees that grow them?' asked Mister Jinky.

'I know lots of *horse*-chestnut trees,' said Meddle. 'You know – the kind we call "conkers" when they fall to the ground and split open their prickly cases – but I don't know any trees that grow eating chestnuts. Do you?'

'Oh, yes,' said Jinky. 'I'll tell you. You know the Bluebell Wood, don't you?'

'Yes,' said Meddle.

'Well, go right through it till you come to the big oak tree in the middle,' said Jinky. 'Then turn to the right, go down the little path there, and you'll soon come to two or three big eating-chestnut trees.'

'How shall I know them?' asked Meddle. 'They are not like horse-chestnuts, are they?'

'Not a bit,' said Jinky. 'You'll know them, my dear Meddle, because they are growing the eating chestnuts you love!'

'Are they in prickly cases like the conkers?' said Meddle.

'They are in cases, but much, much more

prickly ones than the conkers,' said Jinky. 'What a lot of questions you ask, Meddle.'

'Well, I want to be sure I don't make a mistake,' said Meddle. 'I'm always making mistakes – and I'm trying not to now.'

Well, that afternoon Meddle took his biggest basket and set off to Bluebell Wood. He took the little path to the right when he came to the oak tree, and very soon he arrived at the three chestnut trees. Their

leaves were quite different from the conker trees he knew – but Meddle couldn't help knowing they were the right trees, because under them were scattered heaps and heaps of eating chestnuts, some still in their prickly brown cases, and others tumbled out, dark brown and shiny.

'My word, I shall have a lovely lot to take home and roast!' said Meddle, pleased. He began to gather them up and put them into his basket.

'What nice big ones there are!' thought Meddle. 'And oh, my goodness me, look at *that* one!'

Now the one that Meddle was looking at wasn't a chestnut in a case at all. It was a small, brown, prickly hedgehog that had wandered up. As soon as it saw Meddle it had curled itself up tightly, so that it was nothing but a round ball of prickles. There it lay on the ground, perfectly still, looking for all the world like a very big chestnut case, all prickly.

Meddle picked it up. The prickles hurt his fingers, so he soon dropped it into the basket. 'What a giant chestnut must be inside this prickly case!' he thought. 'I'll open it when I get home, and see what kind of a chestnut

there is there. Maybe there are two or three.
What a find!'

He carried his basket home. The hedgehog
didn't move at all. It was frightened. It knew
that as long as it stayed tightly curled up,
nobody could harm it. So there it lay in the
basket, looking just like a big prickly
chestnut.

When Meddle got home he was hungry. 'I
really think I will roast a few chestnuts at
once,' he said. 'I feel as if I could eat a whole
lot. I'll open this great big one first and see
how many nuts there are inside it.'

But, of course, he couldn't open it! The
more he tried, the more tightly the hedgehog
curled itself up. And Meddle pricked his
fingers so badly that they began to bleed.

'You horrid chestnut!' said Meddle, crossly.
'I'll just put you straight down beside the fire
as you are – and you'll have to open then, and
I'll get your nuts!'

So down beside the fire went the
hedgehog, along with a handful of nuts.
Meddle sat down to watch them roast.

Now the hedgehog didn't like the fire at all.
It was much too hot. It lay and thought what
would be the best thing to do. It didn't want

to be cooked. It didn't want to open itself and be caught. But as the fire felt hotter and hotter, the poor hedgehog knew there was only one thing to do – and at once!

'I must crawl away, I really must!' it thought. So it opened out a little, put out its funny little snout, and began to crawl away from the hearth.

Meddle suddenly saw it. He thought he must be dreaming. He rubbed his eyes and looked again. The hedgehog was still crawling.

'My chestnut's walking!' yelled Meddle. Then he saw the little creature's nose, and he gave a yell.

'My chestnut's got a nose! It's got eyes! Goodness, gracious, it's grown legs, too!'

The hedgehog tried to get over the hearthrug. Meddle gave another yell and rushed out of the house. He bumped into Jinky, and held on to him tight.

'*Now* what's the matter?' said Jinky in surprise.

'My big chestnut is walking on the hearthrug!' cried Meddle.

'Don't be silly,' said Jinky.

'And it's got a nose,' said Meddle, clinging

to Jinky, for he really felt very frightened.

'You must be mad,' said Jinky. 'Whoever heard of a chestnut with a nose?'

'And it's got eyes and legs too,' said poor Meddle. 'Oh, Jinky, it must be magic. Oh, I don't like it.'

'I'll come and see this peculiar chestnut,' said Jinky. So he went into Meddle's house and looked around. But the hedgehog had heard him coming and had curled itself up tightly under a chair.

Jinky looked at it. 'There is is!' said Meddle,

pointing. 'But how funny – it hasn't got eyes, or a nose or legs, any more.'

Jinky knew at once that it was a hedgehog. How he grinned to himself! 'We'll soon make it grow eyes and nose and legs again,' he said. 'Get me a saucer of bread and milk for your giant chestnut, Meddle.'

'Bread and milk for a chestnut to eat!' said Meddle, in the greatest surprise. 'Whatever are you talking about?'

'Go and get it,' said Jinky. So Meddle went to his larder and soon came back with a saucer of bread and milk. Jinky set it down beside the tightly curled hedgehog. The hedgehog smelt the food. It uncurled itself. Out came a little nose.

Meddle gave a squeal. 'Look! It's come alive again!'

The hedgehog went to the saucer on its short little legs and began to eat the bread and milk. Meddle watched in the greatest surprise, his eyes nearly falling out of his head.

When the hedgehog had finished the bread and milk, Jinky took out his handkerchief. He wrapped it round the little prickly creature, and lifted it up. The prickles were caught in the handkerchief and did not hurt him.

'If you don't want this giant chestnut, I'll have it,' he said.

'Take it with pleasure!' cried Meddle. 'I don't want such a peculiar thing in my house. You seem to know what to do with it, anyway.'

'Well, I've always liked hedgehogs,' said Jinky with a grin. 'They eat all the slugs and grubs in the garden! I never heard of anybody but gipsies trying to roast a hedgehog before! Another of your little mistakes, I'm afraid, Meddle!'

And off he went, grinning so broadly that his smile reached each of his ears. Well, well, well – what will old Meddle do next? I simply can't imagine, can you?

Chapter 6

Mister Meddle and the Kangaroo

Once upon a time there was a travelling circus that passed near to the town where Mister Meddle lived. Mister Meddle didn't know anything about it, because the circus didn't stop.

But, as it went by the town, the performing kangaroo escaped from its cage! Nobody saw it go. It found that its door hadn't been locked, so it just pushed it open and went out. It hopped right over the nearby hedge with one bound and then jumped in glee over three fields and a stream.

Now, Mister Meddle was just out for his morning walk. He was trying to make up a poem that went like this:

> 'The wind was soft and warm,
> The sky was very blue,
> The birds were singing sweet . . .'

Mister Meddle got as far as those three lines and there he stuck. He just simply could *not* think of a fourth line.

He began again

> 'The wind was soft and warm,
> The sky was very blue,
> The birds were singing sweet –
> IS THAT A KANGAROO?'

Now Mister Meddle didn't mean the last line to rhyme like that, and it really sounded very funny. But he didn't think about its being funny – all he thought about was the very peculiar sight in front of him. Jumping down the field path was a large kangaroo!

Mister Meddle was not used to meeting kangaroos in the fields. He stood still and stared at it.

'Now, I must think about this,' said Mister Meddle. 'Kangaroos don't live in this country.

Therefore that can't be a kangaroo. On the other hand, it's not a rabbit or a hedgehog. And it does really look extremely like a kangaroo.'

The kangaroo bounded nearer. It jumped right over a hedge and back again. Meddle began to feel a little scared. He didn't know how to treat kangaroos. Did you pat them like a dog? Or stroke them like a cat? Or prod them like a pig?

'Now I really *must* think about this,' said Meddle firmly. 'That *is* a kangaroo, but it can't be a real one. So I must be dreaming.

Of course – that's what it is! I'm asleep and dreaming. It's only a dream kangaroo. Well, I'm not frightened of a dream kangaroo. Not a bit! Ho – I've only got to wake up and it will be gone.'

The kangaroo bounded almost on top of Meddle, and stared at him in rather a fierce manner. Meddle stared back.

'Stare all you like!' he said to the kangaroo. 'But let me tell you this – you're not real! Not a bit real. You're only a dream! My dream! Ha ha, ho ho!'

The kangaroo put its face near to Meddle's and made a horrid sort of noise. Meddle jumped back a little.

'If you do that sort of thing to me I'll wake up and then you'll be gone like a puff of smoke!' he said. 'Do you want to be gone? Just be careful, please. I don't like you very much, and I may wake up with a jump. Then you'll be gone for ever.'

'Grr-rrr-rrr-rrr!' said the kangaroo, and put up its fists as if it were going to fight Meddle. It was a very clever kangaroo, and could box with its fists just like a man. It often boxed with its keeper, and it really thought that Meddle would enjoy boxing too.

But Meddle didn't like boxing at all. He stepped back a bit further. The kangaroo followed.

'*Will* you keep away from me?' roared Meddle, getting angry. 'You're a most annoying dream. I'll slap you if you keep following me. Now, I'm going to turn my back on you, and walk away. Maybe when I turn round you'll have changed into a pig or a cat or something, like things always do in dreams. So just look out!'

Meddle turned his back and walked away, hoping and hoping that the kangaroo would turn into a harmless mouse. But no sooner had he walked two steps than he felt a tremendous punch on his right shoulder. He nearly fell over.

He turned round in a rage. The kangaroo was dancing about all round him, aiming at him with its fists, enjoying itself very much. Meddle shouted at it.

'What do you want to punch me like that for? You might have woken me up! You know I'm asleep and dreaming, don't you? I wish I could wake up. You're a very horrid dream.'

The kangaroo gave him another punch, right in his middle this time. Meddle bent

over with a groan. 'You horrid creature! You don't know how to play fair, even! Take that – and that.'

Meddle hit out at the kangaroo, who was simply delighted. He gave Meddle such a punch that the poor man went right through the hedge and out at the other side! Two men were coming over the field there and they stared in great surprise at Meddle flying through the hedge.

'Do you usually come through hedges like that?' asked one of the men, at last.

'Of course not, said Meddle. 'I'm having a very nasty dream, that's all. I can't imagine why you've come into my dream too. Really, I do wish I *could* wake up! I've already dreamt a kangaroo, and he keeps punching me.'

'Dreamt a kangaroo!' cried one of the men. 'Why, we are looking for a kangaroo! Where is he?'

'Oh, for goodness' sake don't call him!' said Meddle. 'He's gone out of my dream for a moment and I really don't want him back.'

'You must be mad,' said one of the men. 'You're not dreaming! You're wide awake.'

'Now look here – I met a kangaroo just now, and I should never do that if I was awake,' said Meddle. 'I tell you, I'm dreaming. Pinch me, please. You can't feel pinches in dreams. Pinch me hard. I shan't feel it, and then you'll know I'm in a dream.'

The men pinched Meddle as hard as they could. He gave a loud yell. 'Ow! Don't! You're hurting me!'

'Well, there you are!' said the men. 'You're not dreaming! Now – where's our kangaroo? He's escaped from our travelling circus.'

Meddle stared at the men with his mouth wide open in surprise and horror. 'Do you mean to say that was a real live kangaroo I saw?' he said at last. 'I didn't dream him? Good gracious, I hit him! He might have eaten me up!'

The men laughed. 'He wouldn't have done that,' they said. 'But you were mighty brave to hit him. He's very strong, and can be quite fierce. Look – here he comes, over the hedge!'

Sure enough, there was the kangaroo, leaping high over the hedge. He jumped to the men, and put his big arms round the one who was his keeper.

'Shake hands with this gentleman,' the keeper said to the kangaroo. But Meddle wasn't going to have any more to do with kangaroos at all! He fled through the hedge again and tore home as fast as he could.

But you should have heard him boasting the next day!

'I was walking along making up a poem,' he told his friends. 'This was the poem:

> 'The wind was soft and warm,
> The sky was very blue,
> The birds were singing sweet . . .
> IS THAT A KANGAROO?'

'But why did you put a kangaroo suddenly into your poem?' asked his friends.

'Because there *was* one, an escaped one!' said Meddle.' Ah, you should have seen me! I went up to him. I ordered him to come with me, and when he wouldn't, I fought him. Slap, bang. I hit him hard. When his keepers came, I handed over the kangaroo to them at once. I shouldn't be surprised if they asked me to join their circus.'

But Meddle didn't tell anyone at all that he had thought the kangaroo was a dream. Wasn't he funny?

Chapter 7

Mister Meddle Makes Another Mistake

Once Mister Meddle felt rather gloomy, and he went about with such a long face that his friends teased him about it.

'Whatever is the matter?' they asked. 'Have you lost a pound and found fifty pence?'

'Don't be silly,' said Mister Meddle. 'I am sad because I am bored.'

'Look here, Meddle,' said Gobo at once, 'you haven't enough to do! That's what's the matter with *you*! You get a job of some kind – or go round helping people. That's the best cure for being bored or sad.'

'Is it really?' said Mister Meddle. 'Well, I'll do that then. I see that Biscuit, the grocer, wants another errand boy. Perhaps I could take that job.'

So off he went to Mr Biscuit, and the grocer said yes, he could be an errand boy.

'What have I to do?' asked Meddle, quite excited.

'Nothing much, except to take parcels round,' said Biscuit. 'This is Sam Quickly, my other errand boy. He's a good lad. You can help him today for a start.'

Well, as you know, Meddle was a muddler – and as Sam Quickly was just like his name, the two didn't get on very well together.

Sam did everything smartly and quickly – but old Meddle fell over sacks, trod on spilt potatoes instead of picking them up, and covered himself with flour almost at once.

'Good gracious! You look like a miller!' said Sam with a giggle. 'Here, take this parcel to Mrs Brown's, and for goodness' sake dust yourself before you go!'

Meddle dusted himself so hard that the flour flew all over the place and Sam sneezed. Then Meddle took the parcel and went off to Mrs Brown's.

But it was a very long way and before long

Meddle began to puff and pant. When a bus came along he hopped into it.

'I shall wear out all my shoes if I walk so far,' said Meddle, sitting down with a sigh. 'How tired my feet are already!'

The bus was full. An old lady got in and glared at Meddle because he had put his parcel down beside him, so that there was hardly any room for her.

'Move that parcel!' she said sharply.

'Sorry,' said Meddle, and he picked up the parcel. He decided to sit on it, then there would be plenty of room. So he sat down on it. It made rather a peculiar noise, but that didn't worry Meddle. No, he just sat there happily.

Then he began to feel rather wet. He looked down at the seat and to his horror he found something bright yellow was dripping off the seat to the floor! The yolk of eggs! Good gracious – surely there weren't eggs in that parcel!

He got up in a hurry – and the parcel stuck to him! Meddle undid the paper quickly – and there, in the parcel, was a bag of twelve broken eggs, a bag of flour soaked with the eggs, a split bag of sugar, and half a pound of butter! The butter looked very strange indeed, for Meddle was quite heavy.

'Bother!' said Meddle. He picked up the spoilt parcel and got off the bus. He ran all the way back to Mr Biscuit's and showed him the parcel.

'How was I to know there were eggs in it?' he said. 'They have spoilt my trousers!'

'Serves you right,' said Mr Biscuit angrily.

'What do I care about your trousers! Nothing at all! What I *do* care about is that you have spoilt Mrs Brown's goods. Sam! Sam! Make up another parcel for Mrs Brown and take it yourself. This poor, silly creature thinks parcels are to be sat on, not delivered.'

Mister Meddle was angry. How dare Mr Biscuit talk about him like that! He made up his mind to show him what he could do when he tried. Poor, silly creature indeed!

'Make up two ounces of pepper for Mrs Jones,' said the grocer to Meddle. 'And look sharp about it! It's in that drawer there.'

Meddle went to the big drawer where the pepper was kept. It was lined with tin, and there was a scoop inside for measuring out the pepper.

Just as Meddle was taking up the scoop to measure the pepper, a large bluebottle came buzzing around. Now, Meddle simply hated bluebottles. He hated their buzz, and he hated their great fat bodies.

'I'll pepper you if you come near me!' said Meddle fiercely. 'Keep away!'

The bluebottle at once flew round Meddle's head. 'Zz-zz-zz-zz!' it said boldly. 'Zz-zz-zz-zz!'

'All right!' said Meddle, in a rage. 'I'll pepper you then!'

He threw a scoopful of pepper at the bluebottle. It flew off and came back again. 'Zz-zz-zz-zz! Zz-zz-zz-zz!'

'Get away, I tell you, get away!' yelled Meddle. He threw another lot of pepper at the bluebottle – and most unfortunately he didn't see Mr Biscuit coming by, and the poor grocer found pepper flying all round him. He glared at Meddle and began to shout at him – and then he sneezed, and sneezed, and sneezed!

'You bad fellow –' he began, 'you – a-tishoo! A-tish-oo! You bad – a-tishoo! Wait till I get you. A-tishoo!' Some customers came in and they began to sneeze too. How they sneezed! They sneezed so much that they had to go out of the shop without buying anything, and that made Mr Biscuit crosser than ever. He gave the surprised Meddle a good scolding.

'Stop playing about with the pepper!' he cried. 'Go out and ask Sam to give you another job in the yard!'

So out went Meddle, sneezing hard himself. Sam was already back from Mrs

Brown's, and he looked in surprise at the sneezing Meddle.

'Got a cold?' he asked. 'Good gracious, what a sneeze you've got – sounds like fireworks going off! Now come along and do some work. All these sacks of goods have got to be taken to the storehouse down the road, where Mr Biscuit keeps a good many things.

Meddle looked at the sacks. Well, that seemed easy enough. He could carry a sack as well as anyone. Here goes! Up went a sack on his shoulder, and Meddle staggered off down the yard, out of the gate, and off to the shed down the road.

The sack was full of potatoes. It was very heavy. Meddle was glad to put it down when he reached the shed. He made up his mind that he wouldn't choose potatoes again – no, not he! He would choose a bag of sago or something that was much lighter.

Sam didn't seem to feel the weight of the sacks at all. He was a good and cheerful worker and he went up and down with the sacks, whistling merrily.

Meddle went round the sacks to feel which ones were the lightest of all. He chose a light one and went off with it. That was better! The next time he again chose a light sack, so that Sam had to take all the heavy ones.

'Look here,' said Sam at last, 'I'm carrying all the heavy ones and you're picking the light ones. That won't do!'

'All right. I'll take a heavy one this time,' said Meddle, and he picked up a sack that he knew was very, very light indeed. It was full of new sponges, dry and light as feathers! But Meddle pretended that it was very heavy

indeed, and groaned as he lifted the sack to his shoulder.

Sam knew the sack was full of dry sponges. He knew it wasn't heavy – Meddle was just pretending. Sam was about to shout at Meddle when something fell on his head – a big drop of rain. Then Sam grinned and said nothing at all. It was going to rain, was it? Well, let Meddle take the sponges then, and see what happened! He'd be rather surprised!

Meddle went off with the sack of sponges, smiling. Aha! He had the lightest sack of all, as light as a feather! It wouldn't take him long to run down the street with *that*!

It began to rain heavily. Thunder crashed overhead and the rain became so heavy that a little rivulet trickled down Meddle's nose and ran off the end.

Now you know what happens to your sponge when you fill it with water – it gets very heavy and very wet! Meddle had a whole *sackful* of sponges – and they began to get very wet indeed!

The wetter they got with the rain, the heavier they felt. Meddle was carrying a whole rainstorm in those sponges! He staggered along with the sack, which got heavier and heavier every minute. Meddle couldn't understand it!

'Now how can a sack change from light to heavy without my putting anything into it?' he said to himself. 'I can't understand it!'

The rain fell more heavily, and the sponges in the sack soaked up the pelting drops and almost dragged Meddle down to the ground. He staggered along, his knees bending under him. Behind him came Sam Quickly, squealing with laughter, for he knew exactly what was happening.

At last the sponges were so heavy and so big with rain that the sack could no longer hold them. It burst – and Meddle was buried under a pile of great wet sponges! When the wet, cold, slithery things slid over him, Meddle gave a yell.

'What is it – what is it? What have I been carrying? Frogs? Toads? Fish? Oh, they've come alive and they are out of the sack! Help, help!'

Meddle scrambled up and rushed home in great fright. Sam Quickly laughed so much that he had to put his own sack down and wipe his eyes. Then he squeezed out the sponges and fetched a fresh sack for them.

'That's the last we'll see of our new errand boy!' said Sam to himself. 'And a good thing too!'

He was right. Meddle didn't go near Mr Biscuit's again. He sat by the fire to dry his things and looked gloomily into the flames.

'Well, work's all right for some people,' said Meddle to himself, 'but it's no good for me. I've got too many brains to be an errand boy!'

It's a great pity that Mr Biscuit doesn't sell brains – if he did, Sam Quickly would buy some and deliver them at Meddle's house, I'm sure!

Chapter 8

Mister Meddle's Umbrella

When Mister Meddle went to stay with his Aunt Jemima, she was very strict with him. She made him put on galoshes when it was wet, and a hat when it was sunny, and a scarf round his throat when the wind was cold.

'I wish you wouldn't fuss!' Meddle kept saying. 'Aunt Jemima, I wish you wouldn't FUSS!'

'Meddle, you are so silly that I'm sure I don't know what would happen to you if I didn't fuss,' said his aunt. 'I am *not* going to have you in bed with colds while you are staying here – so I am going to fuss all I like, and you will have to do as you are told.'

Now if there was one thing more than

anything that Meddle hated, it was taking an
umbrella out with him. He simply couldn't
bear it.

'If I have to carry an umbrella it's a perfect
nuisance!' he said. 'It gets between my ankles
and trips me up. It digs itself into people as I
pass them, and they get angry with me. I just
can't bear an umbrella.'

'Well, my dear Meddle, you'll have to take
one this afternoon when you go out, because
it's simply pouring with rain!' said his aunt
firmly. 'Look at it – pouring cats and dogs.'

'I wish it really *would* pour cats and dogs,'

said Meddle. 'I've always wanted to see that, and I never have. I shan't go out this afternoon, Aunt Jemima, if you make me take an umbrella.'

'Very well,' said his aunt. 'Then you can't call at the book shop and get your *Sunny Stories.*'

'Oh, I simply *must* have that,' said Meddle. 'Why, I might be in the book this week.'

Well, it was still raining that afternoon when Meddle put his coat on, and told Aunt Jemima he was going out. His aunt went to the hall stand and fetched her umbrella. It was a fat red one, and had a bright red, crooked handle. She gave it to him.

'You'll get wet through if you don't take this,' she said. 'Go along now. Hurry up!'

'Bother!' said Meddle. 'Bother, bother, bother. I do so hate umbrellas.'

'Meddle, if you don't take it, you don't go out!' said Aunt Jemima. So Meddle took it, and went down the garden path. He began thinking about a story he was going to write. It was to be about a soldier who was very brave.

'He shall have a sword,' said Meddle to himself. 'An enormous sword. And he will use it like this – slash, slash, poke, poke, slash, slash!'

Meddle began to slash about with the umbrella as if it were a sword. My, he did feel grand. People stared at him in surprise as they passed, but Meddle didn't even see them.

'My soldier shall fight well!' he cried. 'Slash, slash!'

He nearly knocked old Mrs Jinks's hat off her head, and she scurried away in fright. Meddle went all the way to the bookshop in the pouring rain, pretending that the umbrella was a sword. He didn't even put it up. He soon was quite soaked, and the rain dripped down his neck.

So, of course, when he got home again, his coat was dripping and his hair was so wet that it looked dreadful.

'Meddle! Didn't you put up your umbrella?' cried his aunt angrily. 'Oh, you silly creature! What's the use of taking out an umbrella if you don't put it up? Now you will get a dreadful cold.'

'A-tish-oo!' said Meddle, with a sneeze. And the next day he was in bed, feeling very bad.

Well, when he was up, and wanted to go out

for a walk, his Aunt Jemima looked up at the sky. 'Meddle,' she said, 'it looks like rain. I don't think I can trust you to go out. You'll only get wet again.'

'Aunt Jemima, if only you'll let me go out and buy a bag of boiled sweets, I promise I'll take an umbrella,' said Meddle.

'But will you put it up?' asked his aunt. 'You took an umbrella last time, but you didn't put it up. And what's the use of that? Last time you said your umbrella was a sword. This time you may pretend it's a lamp post or something.'

Well, Meddle got his way. He took the fat red umbrella out of the hall stand and went off. It wasn't raining, but after a little some drops began to fall. Meddle was busy putting his hand into the bag to get out a nice red sweet, and he was cross.

'Stupid rain!' he said. 'Well, I promised my aunt to put up the umbrella, so I must.'

Meddle held up his umbrella above his head, but he didn't put it up! He just held it up like a stick, without opening the umbrella at all. He was so busy with his sweets that he forgot that an umbrella must be opened when it is held up. So there he was, going down the road, getting wetter and wetter, his umbrella held unopened above his head.

'Well, well,' said Meddle to himself. 'What's the use of an umbrella, after all, I'd like to know? I'm getting just as wet as if I'd not taken one with me at all. Splash, splash, splash, the rain comes down – and I'm getting soaked.'

Now Aunt Jemima was watching for Meddle when he came home – and when she saw him walking up the path with his umbrella held

like a stick over his head, she was really very angry. Meddle saw her frowning and he was puzzled.

'Now what's the matter, Aunt?' he cried, as he walked up the path and saw her looking out of the window. 'I took the umbrella, didn't I? And I put it up, didn't I? But what's the use – I'm just as wet as ever!'

'My dear Meddle, you might as well take a toothpick to hold over your head as an umbrella, if you don't bother to put it up,' said his aunt. 'Look up and see your umbrella.'

So Meddle looked up, and saw that he had forgotten to open the umbrella, and he felt rather foolish. 'Dear me,' he said. 'I've been rather silly.'

'You'll have a cold tomorrow,' said Aunt Jemima.

'A-tish-oo!' said Meddle. And, of course, he was in bed with a cold the very next day.

Well, well. Aunt Jemima was very cross and not a bit nice to Meddle. When he was up again, she spoke to him very sternly.

'Meddle, every time you go out in future you will take an umbrella with you,' she said. 'And you will practise putting it up and down, up and down, before you go out. Then perhaps you will remember that an umbrella is meant to be opened when it is in use.

So Meddle practised putting the umbrella up and down, and opened and shut it a dozen times before he went out. The cat hated it. It was a great shock to her whenever Meddle suddenly opened the umbrella just in front of her.

When Meddle's cold was better enough for him to go out, his aunt made him take the umbrella with him.

'But it isn't raining!' said Meddle. 'No, Aunt, I'd look silly.'

'You'll look a lot sillier if you get a third cold, and miss your birthday party,' said Aunt Jemima. 'Take the umbrella, and don't make a fuss, Meddle.

So Meddle took it with him, though the sun was shining brightly. He went to visit his friend Gobo, and he sat and talked to him for a long time. And, of course, when he left to go home, he quite forgot to take the umbrella with him. He left it behind in Gobo's hall-stand!

And when he was almost home the rain came down. How it poured! You should have seen it. Meddle got quite a shock when he felt the big raindrops stinging his face.

'Ha! Good thing I took an umbrella with me!' he said. 'A very good thing indeed. I'll put it up.'

But the umbrella wasn't there to put up. Meddle stared all round as if he thought the umbrella would come walking up. But of course it didn't.

'Bother!' said Meddle. 'Where's it gone? I know I had it when I left home. How can I put an umbrella up if it isn't here? My goodness! What will Aunt Jemima say when she sees me coming home in the rain without the umbrella? I wonder if she's looking out of the window. I won't peep and see in case she is. I'll run all the way back to Gobo's and see if I've left the umbrella there!'

If only Meddle had looked he would have seen his aunt knocking at the window to tell him to run quickly up the garden path and come in out of the rain! Instead of that, he ran down the road again, and went all the way back to Gobo's with the rain pouring down on him. How wet he got! He dripped like a piece of seaweed.

By the time he got to Gobo's he was wet

through and shivering. He banged at the door. Gobo opened it.

'I've come back for my umbrella before I get wet,' said Meddle.

'You silly! You're soaked already,' said Gobo. 'As for your umbrella, I've sent Mrs Gobo to your aunt's with it. You must have missed her. I can't lend you one because I haven't one at the moment. My goodness, won't you get wet!'

So Meddle had to run back in the rain without an umbrella at all, and his shoes went squelch, squelch, squelch, and his coat went drip, drip, drip.

How angry his Aunt Jemima was when he came in. 'Meddle! I send you out with an umbrella, and you come home in the pouring rain without it, and I knock at the window to tell you to come in, and you run off down the road again, and then Mrs Gobo comes in with your umbrella, and you come home again as wet as a sponge. You'll get a very bad cold.'

'A-tish-oo!' said Meddle at once. 'A-tish-oo! I must go and get a hanky!'

And, of course, he was in bed with a bad cold the next day and missed his birthday party after all! Now he is packing up to go home because his aunt says she won't keep him any longer. Do you know what she gave him for a birthday present? Guess! An umbrella – and the handle is a donkey's head.

'I chose a donkey because I really thought it would suit you well,' said Aunt Jemima.

But I expect he will leave it in the bus, don't you?

Chapter 9

Mister Meddle Does a Bit of Good

Once there came a magician to Meddle's village. He was very clever, and knew a great deal of magic. His name was Sneaky, and he was just like his name.

He was not a nice person. He was mean to everybody, and they couldn't be mean back, because they were afraid of him. They stayed in their houses when Sneaky came by, because they were so afraid he might take them to be his servants.

But, of course Meddle didn't stay in *his* house. Oh no! – he was far too curious about Sneaky. He longed to see what he was like. So when he knew that the magician was coming down the road, Meddle hopped out of his front door and squeezed himself inside a bush, so that he might peep out at Sneaky.

Sneaky wore very soft shoes that made no sound. Meddle couldn't hear him coming at all. 'I must peep out and see if he has gone by,' said Meddle at last. So he poked out his head – and just at that very moment Sneaky came by! He saw Meddle peeping out of the bush and he stopped and grinned.

'Ho! Spying on me! This won't do, my dear fellow, this won't do!'

'I'm s-s-s-s-orry!' said Meddle, shivering in his shoes. 'I j-j-j-just wanted to s-s-s-see what you were l-l-l-like!'

'Oh, you wanted to see what I was like, did you?' said Sneaky. 'Well, you just come home with me, and you'll soon see what I am like! I need a servant.'

And to Meddle's dismay Sneaky reached out a long arm, picked him out of the bush, tucked him under his arm like a parcel and went off with him.

'Well, it serves Meddle right,' said everyone, peeping from their windows. 'He is always prying and meddling!'

Poor Meddle! He didn't like being the

magician's servant at all. He wasn't very good at cooking. He wasn't very good at cleaning. He didn't remember anything he was told, and he was always poking his nose into the magician's books and spells.

'One day you'll leave your nose behind you, if you poke it into any more of my magic,' said Sneaky angrily, when he found Meddle reading one of his magic books. 'Go about your work. Clean my broomsticks today, and all the furniture too. It looks dreadful! Look at those smears! Look at those stains!'

'Y-y-y-yes, sir,' said Meddle. 'B-b-but I haven't any more p-p-p-polish.'

'What a nuisance you are!' said Sneaky. 'Always wanting some more of this, and some more of that. I will give you some polish today – and you must make it last for a whole week.'

Sneaky went to a cupboard. He took out two tins. One was blue and one was green.

'Now listen carefully,' he said sternly to Meddle. 'This blue tin is for my broomsticks. It is a fly-away polish, and has magic in it, so that when I want to use my broomsticks to fly away on, they will go smoothly and swiftly through the air. And this polish, in the green

tin, is a good, bright polish for the furniture.
Now go away and work hard.'

'Yes, sir,' said Meddle, and he took the tins
of polish. He went to the kitchen. He sighed
deeply. He hated polishing. He looked at the
clock – four o'clock, tea-time!

'I really must have a cup of tea first,' said
Meddle. Just then he heard the front door
bang, and he ran to the window. 'Ha! There's
old Sneaky going out! Good! Now I can have
a cup of tea in peace.

He made himself a pot of tea. He sat back
on a chair, put his feet on a stool, and took up

his cup. Ah, this was nice – almost like being at home!

But just then he heard the sound of a key being slid into a lock – Sneaky was back again already! Meddle leapt up in a great hurry, spilt the tea all down himself, and rushed to get his polishing cloths. If Sneaky found him lazing instead of polishing, how angry he would be!

Meddle opened the two tins of polish. He stole quietly into the dining-room, where Sneaky kept his magic broomsticks. Then he looked at the tins of polish.

'Goodness!' said Meddle, scratching his head. 'Now which was which? Was the blue tin the fly-away polish, or the green?'

He simply *couldn't* remember. He didn't dare to go and ask. He stood there and stared at both tins.

'Well, *I* think Sneaky said the green polish was for his broomsticks, and the blue polish was for the furniture,' said Meddle at last. 'I'll do the broomsticks first.'

He began to polish the broomsticks with the green polish. They shone and glittered. Meddle did all six of the broomsticks, and then turned to the furniture. He dabbed his cloth into the tin of blue polish. It was the fly-away polish, of course, but Meddle didn't think it was.

'I'll polish Sneaky's oak chair first,' said Meddle to himself. 'That's about the most important piece of furniture in the room.'

So he began to polish the big armchair with the blue polish. My word, how that chair shone and gleamed! It was marvellous polish. And it was magic too – for whoever sat down in that chair would now fly away in it, goodness knew where.

'Oooh, I'm tired,' said Meddle at last. 'My arm aches. I must have a little rest. I'll pretend to be Sneaky and sit down in his chair. How important I shall feel!'

Meddle was just about to sit down in Sneaky's chair, when the magician himself came into the room. How he glared at Meddle!

'What! You are daring to sit in my chair!' he cried. 'Get out at once!'

He pushed Meddle so hard that the poor fellow went spinning into a corner, and fell over all the broomsticks there. They tumbled across him with a clatter.

'Ha ha!' laughed Sneaky, sitting down hard

in his char. 'How funny you look, Meddle!'

But his laughter soon stopped, and a frightened look came on his face. His chair was rising into the air! 'Hi! What's this? Stop, stop!' yelled Sneaky. But the chair didn't stop. It flew up to the ceiling. Bang! It made a hole there! It flew through the hole, up, up to the roof!

'You wicked meddler, you've polished my chair with the fly-away polish!' yelled Sneaky in a rage. 'Wait till I jump out and catch you!'

But it was too late for him to jump out.

Crash! The chair flew through the roof, and a shower of tiles fell down. Meddle stared in the greatest surprise. He ran to the door and looked upwards. There was Sneaky flying away in the old oak chair – up, up, up to the clouds! He got smaller and smaller, the further he went.

'Ooooh,' said Meddle, hardly believing his eyes. He sat down on the grass and wiped his forehead. 'Ooooooh. He's gone. Simply gone. Just like that! And all because I used the wrong polish. Well, well, well! It seems as if it's a good thing to be silly sometimes!'

The folk in Meddle's village saw the curious sight of Sneaky flying through the roof of his house, away up to the sky. They came running to Sneaky's house, and there they saw Meddle sitting on the grass.

'What's happened? What's happened?' they cried.

'Well, you see, I polished Sneaky's chair with the wrong polish,' explained Meddle. 'I used the fly-away polish instead of the furniture polish. I am always so foolish.'

'Why, Meddle, that was the cleverest thing you've ever done!' cried everyone.

'But I didn't mean to be clever,' said

Meddle honestly. 'It was a mistake!'

'Good old Meddle, fine old Meddle!' cried everyone, and they all crowded round him and shook hands.

'Come to tea with me tomorrow,' said one.

'Come and have some of my ripe plums,' said another.

'Come and have a cup of cocoa with me,' said a third.

Meddle was most astonished. He wasn't used to being made a fuss of. He liked it. It was nice.

'Thank you, kind friends,' he said. 'I think that now I've done *one* clever thing, I may perhaps be cleverer in the future. Anyway, I'll try!'

So he's trying, and not getting on so badly either. I'll be sure and tell you if he starts meddling and getting into trouble again.

Chapter 10

You're a Nuisance, Mister Meddle

Once Mister Meddle was going down the lane, past Farmer Corny's apple orchard, when he saw a spire of smoke rising up from the village not far off.

'My!' said Mister Meddle to himself, 'that looks as if someone's house is on fire!'

Three small boys came up, and Mister Meddle spoke to them. 'Have you come from the village? Is anyone's house on fire?'

'Don't know,' said the biggest boy. He turned to look at the spire of smoke. Then he looked at Meddle. Then he looked into the apple orchard, where apples hung ripe and red. He saw there a ladder going up a tree, and at the top of it was Farmer Corny himself, picking apples.

Then the little boy spoke again to Meddle. 'Well, maybe there *is* a house on fire!' he said. 'Maybe there is someone that wants rescuing! Maybe they haven't a ladder to rescue them with! Whatever will they do?'

Meddle thought it would be fine to be a hero and rescue someone from a burning house. He could see himself going up a long ladder, jumping into a smoky window and

coming out with someone over his shoulder. How the crowd would cheer him! How important he would feel!'

'I wish I had a ladder,' said Meddle. 'You can't rescue people from burning houses without a ladder –'

'Look, mister, there's a ladder!' said the naughty little boy, and he pointed to the one in the orchard nearby. 'You could take that one!'

'So I could, so I could!' said Meddle. 'What a sharp little boy you are!'

Meddle jumped over the wall and ran to the ladder. He didn't see the farmer up the tree. He pulled away the ladder and put it over his shoulder.

The farmer saw someone walking off with his ladder and yelled out angrily.

'Hi! Bring that back at once! What do you mean by going off with my ladder?'

'Just going to rescue someone from a burning house!' yelled back Meddle. 'I'll bring it back soon. You go on picking your apples!'

The farmer was very angry, but he couldn't get down from the tree because the branches were so high above the ground. The little boys gave Meddle a cheer as he went over the wall with the ladder and set off down the lane. He felt quite a hero already.

The naughty little boys saw the farmer was safely up a high tree and couldn't get down. So up into the smaller trees they went and were soon stuffing their pockets with the rosy-red apples. The farmer went purple with rage, but he couldn't do anything about it. He didn't want to break his leg by jumping down to the ground.

Meddle trotted off down to the village. He met Mr Jinky and spoke to him.

'Where's the fire?'

'What fire?' said Jinky.

'The house on fire. I'm going to rescue somebody with this ladder,' said Meddle. 'You know – climb up to a top window.'

'Oh,' said Jinky. 'Well, I should find the fire first if I were you.'

Meddle thought that was a silly remark. He went on his way, looking for the fire. But nobody's house seemed to be on fire. He could still see the spire of smoke rising up in the air, so he went towards it as fast as he could, carrying the heavy ladder over his shoulder.

'Where are you going with that ladder?' asked Dame Trot-About in surprise, when he nearly knocked her over with one end of it.

'Just off to rescue somebody from the burning house!' said Meddle importantly. 'Out of my way, please!'

'What burning house?' asked Dame Trot-About in surprise. But Meddle had gone round the corner, almost knocking down a lamp-post with the long ladder!

At last he came to where the smoke rose high in the air. But oh, what a dreadful disappointment for poor Meddle, it was only the smoke from Mr Smiley's garden bonfire. It was a very, very good bonfire, and the smoke rose high from it. Mr Smiley was piling all kinds of things on it to make it burn well.

'So there isn't a house on fire after all, and there isn't anyone to rescue!' said poor Meddle sadly. Mr Smiley thought Meddle must be mad.

'I don't know what you mean,' he said. 'Why are you taking that heavy ladder about?'

Meddle didn't answer. He turned sadly round, almost knocking one of Mr Smiley's trees down with the end of the ladder, and went back to Farmer Corny's orchard.

As soon as he got there he heard the farmer's angry voice. 'You wait till I catch you young monkeys! Stealing my apples like that! You just wait!'

The naughty boys didn't see Meddle coming back with the ladder. Meddle saw at once what had happened, and he put the ladder back up the farmer's tree. Farmer Corny was down in a second.

Didn't those bad boys get a shock! My goodness me, there was the farmer at the bottom of their tree. And what a scolding they got when they came down. They had to empty their pockets of the apples and off they went howling.

Then the farmer turned to Meddle, who was standing near by watching. 'Good thing I brought the ladder back when I did,' said Meddle, thinking that he had done the farmer a good turn.

'What did you want to take it away for?' cried the farmer, and to Meddle's enormous surprise, he found himself caught by the farmer's huge hand and shaken hard – so hard that his teeth rattled in his head, and he was afraid they would fall out!

'*I'll* teach you to take ladders to rescue

people!' cried the farmer. '*I'll* teach you to let bad boys get into my trees and steal my apples. *I'll* teach you to leave me stuck up a tree for ages!'

He did teach Meddle – for I'm sure he will never, never take a ladder again and go rushing off to rescue people from a burning house that is only a bonfire.

Poor old Meddle!

Chapter 11

Mister Meddle is Rather Foolish

Once upon a time Mister Meddle went on a walking tour with Mr Jinks, his friend. They walked all day long in the summer heat, and got rather tired and very hot and extremely cross.

And then Mr Jinks began to sneeze! Mister Meddle stared at him in amazement.

'Jinks! You don't mean to say you can possibly have caught cold in this hot weather?'

'Well, that's just when you *do* catch cold!' said Jinks, blowing his nose. 'You get very hot – and then take off a lot of clothes – and the wind blows, and hey presto – atishoo – a cold has arrived!'

'How very silly!' said Mister Meddle. 'Well, come on, Jinks. We'll never get to the next village if we don't hurry! I want something to eat – and then we'll go to bed, bed, bed, and rest our poor tired feet.'

'It's a pity we have to use our feet so much on a walking holiday,' groaned Mr Jinks. 'I should enjoy walking so much more if I could go on a bicycle.'

'Don't be silly,' said Meddle.

'That's twice you've said I'm silly,' said Jinks crossly. 'I wish you'd be quiet if you can't say anything more polite.'

'All right,' said Meddle. 'I won't say another word!'

And he didn't, not even when Jinks asked him a question. So by the time they arrived at the next village and looked for an inn they were not the best of friends.

They found a cosy, little inn and went inside. They had a fine supper of ham and eggs, stewed plums, custard and cocoa. After that they both felt so sleepy that they fell asleep in their chairs and didn't wake up till it was dark.

'This *is* silly of us!' groaned Jinks, waking up and yawning. 'Come on, Meddle, let's go to bed. A-tish-oo! A-TISH-OO! Oh, bother this cold!'

'I hope you keep it to yourself and don't give it to me,' said Meddle. 'Hurry up. I've lit the candle.'

They both went upstairs. They had a cosy bedroom with a funny slanting ceiling and a floor that went up and down, it was so uneven.

They undressed and got into bed. 'Isn't it hot?' said Meddle. 'We'd better open the window.'

'Oh no, please don't,' said Jinks, sneezing again. 'I shall get a much worse cold if we have an open window with the wind blowing on us all night long.'

'But, Jinks, I can't sleep if I'm hot,' said Meddle.

'And I can't sleep if I'm cold,' said Jinks firmly. 'And what's more, I'm JOLLY WELL NOT going to have the window open tonight. Do you want me to be too ill in the morning to go on with our walking?'

'Oh, well, please yourself,' said Meddle, getting into bed. 'But I tell you this, Jinks, I am QUITE, QUITE SURE that I shan't be able to go to sleep unless the window is open.'

They both shut their eyes. Jinks sneezed and coughed. Meddle tossed and turned. He felt hotter and hotter and hotter. It was dreadful! Oh, to have the window open and feel a nice cool breeze blowing! He could go to sleep at once then.

'I'm so dreadfully hot,' said Meddle. He breathed very fast to show Jinks how hot he was. 'I almost feel that my tongue will hang out like a dog's soon.'

'Well, if it does, perhaps you'll stop talking

and let *me* get to sleep,' said Jinks crossly.

'Jinks! How perfectly horrid you are!' cried Meddle. 'Oh dear! I'm so hot I must throw all the clothes off.'

'Well, don't throw them off me, too!' said Jinks, clutching at the blankets as Meddle threw them off. 'Oh, do lie down and go to sleep. You're just making a fuss. I could easily go to sleep if only you would.'

'Well, I tell you that I shall never, never, never go to sleep if we don't have the window open,' groaned Meddle.

'Oh, for goodness' sake, open it then,' said Jinks crossly. '*I'll* never go to sleep as long as you lie awake throwing all the clothes off me, and tossing about like a whale trying to catch its dinner.'

'Don't be silly,' said Meddle.

'That's the third time you've said that,' said Jinks fiercely, sitting up in bed. 'If you say it again I'll throw you out of bed.'

'All right, all right,' said Meddle, getting out of bed. 'I'm going to open the window. Wherever is it?'

'Over there,' said Jinks.

'What do you mean, over there?' said Meddle, feeling around. 'There's an awful lot of over theres in this room. But there doesn't seem to be any window.'

'Of course there is,' said Jinks. 'Light the candle and find it.'

'The candle seems to have disappeared, and the matches, too,' said Meddle, feeling about. 'Ah – I believe I've got the window now, I can feel glass!'

'I'm sure the window wasn't there,' said Jinks, in surprise. 'I thought there was a bookcase there or a table or something.'

'Well, you thought wrong,' said Meddle, fumbling round the glass. 'A window is made of glass, isn't it? Well, this is glass, so it's the window. Don't be silly.'

'Meddle! I'll kick you out of bed as soon as you get in!' said Jinks furiously.

'Don't worry. I shan't be in for a long, long time yet,' said Meddle dolefully. 'I can't seem to find out how to open this silly window at all. It just doesn't seem to open at the top or bottom or the side. Oh, I'm getting so ANGRY with it!'

'Tell it not to be silly,' said Jinks.

'Well, I will!' said Meddle, and he spoke angrily to the window. 'Don't be silly, window! If you don't let me open you, I'll smash you and let the fresh air in that way!'

But it was no good. Meddle simply could *not* open the window at all. He got angrier and angrier. And to make things worse, Jinks suddenly began to giggle. How he giggled! He went on and on like a river running down hill. Meddle was simply furious with him.

'Now what in the wide world are you giggling about, Jinks?' he said. 'Is it so funny that I can't open the window?'

'Yes, Meddle – if you only knew what I know, you'd be giggling, too!' chuckled Jinks, stuffing the sheet into his mouth to stop himself from laughing.

'Well, what *do* you know,' said Meddle, slapping his hand against the glass angrily.'

'Shan't tell you,' said Jinks. 'You keep calling me silly – so I'll be silly and not tell you.'

'Well, you're sillier than I even thought you were,' said Meddle in disgust. 'Oh, you awful window! Oh, you horrid thing! Take that – and that – and that!'

Meddle hit out for all he was worth – and there came the sound of breaking glass!

'Ah!' said Meddle. 'I'm glad I've broken you, very glad. You deserved it. Now the fresh

air can come in and I can breathe it and go to sleep. Ahhhh – the lovely fresh air!'

Meddle sniffed and sniffed, thinking how marvellously cool the room had become.

'Don't you feel the lovely fresh air blowing in, Jinks?' he asked.

'No, I don't,' said Jinks.

'What! Can't you feel the cool breeze?' cried Meddle, climbing into bed.

'No, I can't,' said Jinks, and he gave another giggle.

'I simply don't know what's come over you tonight, Jinks,' said Meddle, settling down under the blankets. 'Giggling like that over nothing. You ought to be ashamed of yourself.'

'*You'll* be ashamed of yourself in the morning,' said Jinks, with another helpless giggle.

'I certainly shan't,' said Meddle. 'My word, it's quite cool now that I've broken that window and let in the cold night air. Good night, Jinks, I hope you'll have got over your giggles by the morning.'

Jinks had another fit of giggles, and shook the bed with them. Meddle shut is eyes and was soon asleep. And then Jinks slept too, though once he awoke and began to giggle again.

In the morning Meddle sat up and yawned. He stared at the window. It was fast shut! The glass was not broken at all!

'There's a funny thing!' said Meddle. 'Didn't I break you last night, window?'

Jinks sat up and began to giggle again. He pointed to a bookcase over in the corner. It had a glass front to it that was locked – and some of the glass was smashed!

'Oh, Meddle! You broke that glass-fronted bookcase last night and not the window!' said

Jinks, going off into a laugh. 'I knew you had – that's why I began to giggle. It was so funny the way you kept asking me if I didn't feel the cool air coming in through the broken window – and all the time the window was quite whole and fast shut, and it was the bookcase you had broken!'

'Goodness gracious!' said Meddle, in dismay. 'I'll have to pay a lot of money for that. Well, well – how was it I thought I felt the cold night air coming in, I wonder? I just simply can't understand it!'

'I can!' said Jinks, going off into giggles again. 'You're just a silly, Meddle – just a **GREAT BIG SILLY!**'

And for once poor Meddle couldn't find any answer at all!

Chapter 12

Mister Meddle and the Horse

Now once Farmer Straw was ill, and he was worried about his horse.

'He needs someone to look after him,' he said to his servant, Annie. 'Send for Meddle. Maybe he can keep an eye on him for me. He will need feeding, and watering, and a little canter over the hills now and again.'

So Meddle was sent for and Farmer Straw told him about the horse.

'You keep an eye on him for me,' he said. 'He is a good, well-mannered horse, and won't be any trouble. He is a wise old fellow, is Captain, and he understands every word you say to him.'

'Does he really?' said Meddle, surprised. 'Well, I shan't have much difficulty with him, then. Don't you worry, Farmer Straw, Captain and I will get on well together.'

'There are oats in the bin,' said the farmer. 'And the grooming-brush is in his stable. You'll have to give him water, too, because the field he is in has no stream running through it.'

'Right,' said Meddle, and walked off, feeling most important. He had once looked after a canary, and once looked after his aunt's cat – but he had never looked after such a big animal as a horse before.

'Such a wise old horse, too,' thought Meddle. 'Understands every word said to him. Fancy that! Well, I can ask him what he wants, and he'll know all right.'

Meddle went to the field where Captain was. The horse cantered over to him.

'Hello, Captain,' said Meddle, and patted his nose. 'Do you want a nice drink of water? I can bring you some in a pail, if you do.'

'Nay-ay-ay-ay-ay?' neighed the horse, pleased to hear the word 'water' for he was thirsty.

'Nay?' said Meddle. 'Did you say "nay"? That means no. So you don't want any water. All right. You really are a clever horse. You not only understand what I say to you, but you answer, too.'

Meddle went off to get his dinner. The horse looked after him, disappointed. He wanted some water, but he didn't get it.

After dinner Meddle went back to the horse, which cantered eagerly to the gate.

'Would you like some oats?' asked Meddle.

'Nay-ay-ay-ay-ay!' neighed the horse, in delight. Oats! Just what he would like! The grass in his field was very poor – but oats were good.

'Nay?' said Meddle, surprised. 'Dear me –

fancy not wanting oats. I shouldn't have thought a big hefty horse like you would have said "nay" to oats. I should have thought you would have said "yes".'

He looked at the horse, who nuzzled against him, trying to let him know that he wanted both oats and water. Meddle stroked his soft nose.

'Would you like to come out of your field for a nice little canter?' he said. 'Farmer Straw said you might like a run over the hills.'

'Nay-ay-ay-ay-ay!' neighed the horse at once in delight. Ah – if he could only get out for a canter, he could drink from the first stream he came to. That would be fine.

'What a horse you are for saying no to everything,' said Meddle. 'Don't you want anything at all, Captain? It's no trouble to me to get you anything you want, you know.'

'Nay-ay-ay-ay-ay,' said the old horse.

'All right,' said Meddle. 'If you don't want anything, I won't get it. I'm off to market now. If you're a good horse, maybe I'll bring you back something you'll like.'

He set off for market. He bought all kinds of things there for himself – and he bought a beautiful bunch of early carrots for Captain, the horse. They were very dear, very small, but very sweet.

'Aha! Captain will like these,' thought Meddle to himself. 'He won't say no to these. He'll say "yes-es-es-es-essssss!"'

He went home with his goods. Then he went to the field, carrying behind him the bunch of feather carrots. He spoke to Captain, who nuzzled at him eagerly, smelling the carrots that Meddle hid behind his back.

'Captain, do you want some nice young carrots?' asked Meddle. 'Now, think before you answer!'

'Nay-ay-ay-ay-ay!' neighed the horse in delight. Carrots! How wonderful. But Meddle was cross.

'There you go – saying no to me again!' he said, angrily. 'What a particular horse you are! Nothing I offer you pleases you! You won't have water, oats, a canter or even new carrots! I am disgusted with you. It's nay, nay, nay all the time. Why don't you say yes, yes, yes, for a change?'

He left the poor, hungry, thirsty old horse and went off home. On the way he passed the farmhouse, and the servant saw him. 'Come

in and speak to the master for a minute,' she said. 'He's fretting about his old horse.'

Meddle marched in. The farmer looked at him. 'Meddle, have you fed and watered my horse? Have you taken him for a canter?'

'No,' said Meddle. 'He's a most obstinate horse. He says "nay-nay-nay" to everything I ask him. What's the use of looking after a horse that says no to everything?'

'Meddle, don't you know a horse can only say "nay"?' cried the farmer. 'Are you cruel, or just stupid? Meddle, come here. I think you

351

need a really good scolding. Come here.'

'Nay-ay-ay-ay-ay!' cried Meddle, and you should have seen him run. He went even faster than the old horse. What a silly he is, isn't he?